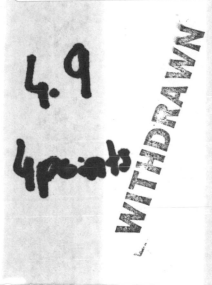

No Strings Attached

Kristi D. Holl

Atheneum   1988   New York

To Linda Callaway,
for her warm friendship with "no strings attached"

Copyright © 1988 by Kristi D. Holl

All rights reserved. No part of this book may be reproduced
or transmitted in any form or by any means, electronic or·
mechanical, including photocopying, recording, or by any
information storage and retrieval system, without permission
in writing from the publisher.

Atheneum
Macmillan Publishing Company
866 Third Avenue, New York, NY 10022
Collier Macmillan Canada, Inc.
Type set by Arcata Graphics/Kingsport, Kingsport, Tennessee
Printed and bound by Fairfield Graphics, Fairfield, Pennsylvania
Designed by Marjorie Zaum
First Edition

10 9 8 7 6 5 4 3 2 1

Library of Congress Cataloging–in–Publication Data

Holl, Kristi.
No strings attached/Kristi D. Holl.—1st ed. p. cm.
SUMMARY: June finds sharing a house with her mother and her
foster grandfather requires a difficult adjustment
to his forgetfulness and his crabby remarks to her
junior high school friends, but she also loves him
as a family member.
ISBN 0–689–31399–3
[1. Grandfather—Fiction. 2. Old Age—Fiction.] I. Title.
PZ7.H7079No 1988
87–22688 CIP AC
[Fic]—dc19

Contents

BOOKS BY KRISTI D. HOLL

No
Strings
Attached

1
Settling In

❦❦❦

*J*une Finch wiped her sweaty face on the corner of her rumpled blouse, collapsed on the braided rug and leaned against the piano, staring at the old man across the living room. It was still hard for June to believe: She'd inherited a new home and a grandfather of her very own, all in one day.

"I'm done," June called as her mom went by. "Where do you want these empty packing boxes?"

"Let's see." Stopping in the living-room doorway, her mom appeared fresh in spite of the afternoon heat. "What do you think, Franklin? Do you want the boxes stored in the basement, or should we just throw them out?"

"Humph," he growled.

Franklin Cooper stared at old photograph albums as

he sat hunched over in a rocking chair by the window. The padded rocker was still covered by a dust sheet, used during the previous year while Franklin was living at Reed's Retirement Ranch and the house had stood empty. Dressed in black from head to toe, Franklin had been in the same slumped position for the past hour.

June lifted her blond hair from the back of her neck. "Franklin, don't you want to take off your sweater? It's so hot." He'd put on the black sweater, thin at the elbows and cuffs, earlier that day. The morning had been cool, but the August afternoon had reached eighty-five degrees. "Franklin?"

When he didn't even grunt an answer, June shrugged and leaned back. Last year, when she'd first visited Franklin as part of a foster grandparent program, he'd ignored her for weeks. At the time, his cold behavior had really bothered her. Now, though, she'd come to expect it. With a wink, her mother left to finish unpacking in the kitchen.

Abruptly, Franklin hurled himself forward out of the chair. He stumbled, then caught himself. "Closet," he mumbled darkly.

With slow steps, he dragged a chair over to the hall door. Gripping the doorjamb with his gnarled fingers, he pulled himself up on top of the chair.

June scrambled to her feet. "Can I help? You probably shouldn't be climbing like that."

Franklin brushed her hand away as if she were a pesky fly. "I don't need help." Scowling, his black bushy eyebrows drew together in a line over his hawk nose. He turned and poked his head deep into the dark closet.

4

June sighed. How he hated to have someone help him!

She should have remembered. They'd been through it a hundred times before. Last year, when he'd lived at the ranch, he'd resented any person who'd tried to help him. Now that June, her mom, and Franklin were all living together in Franklin's house on Brewster Street, June should have realized that things wouldn't be very different.

Shaking her head, June realized she didn't envy her mom's new job as Franklin's paid companion and housekeeper.

Even if Franklin *was* blunt at times, June had to admit they'd grown close over the past year, especially during her mom's illness. June was glad they'd been able to move into Franklin's empty house just before school started, instead of moving to her aunt's home in Cincinnati. It had been a close call, though. Just two short weeks ago, she and her mom had been all set to leave town.

June glanced around the old-fashioned living room. In spite of the cardboard boxes strewn about, it seemed homey already. With all the potted plants Franklin had brought from his apartment at the retirement home, the room resembled a greenhouse. Begonias and violets filled the window ledges, while planters of ivy and ferns hung from all the empty curtain rods.

The worn couch, padded chairs, and tinny upright piano were Franklin's, too. He'd insisted on keeping the furniture just the way it was. So even though the Finches' couch was newer and the springs didn't stick up, they'd put it in storage, along with many of their other things. There simply wasn't room for everything in Franklin's little house.

A *screech* on the bare wood floor made June whirl around. "Look out, Franklin!"

As Franklin stepped down, his hands full of old photos, the chair slid sideways. June grabbed his arm to steady him. Faded yellowed pictures flew from his hands and skidded across the hardwood floor.

Franklin shook off her arm. "Now look what you've done!"

Down on her hands and knees, June gathered the discolored photos. After saving Franklin from a serious fall, she wasn't surprised that that was all the thanks she got.

Anne Finch scurried around the corner. "What happened?"

"Franklin almost fell, but he's okay," June said, crawling to her feet.

"Did not." Franklin snatched the pictures from June. "I was getting down when she almost knocked me over."

June's mouth fell open, then she clamped it shut again. It wouldn't do any good to correct him.

Shuffling down the short hallway toward his bedroom, Franklin's low mumbles reached their ears. "Do what I want. *My* house. Young whippersnapper-know-it-all."

June picked up the overturned chair. "Did you hear him?" she whispered to her mom. "He could have broken his neck a minute ago. Just like last year when he sprained his ankle." One afternoon at the retirement ranch, they'd been identifying wildflowers down by Thunder Creek when he'd slipped on the creek bank and sprained an ankle. "He wouldn't let me help then, either. In fact . . ."

"Shhh!" her mom warned.

Scowling, Franklin was clomping back down the hall. "Junk everywhere," he muttered, kicking a packing box as he went by.

Arm clutched to his chest, he shuffled into the kitchen. Soon they heard rattling sounds and cupboard doors banging.

Anne Finch winked at June. "Try to be patient with Franklin, okay? He's really glad to be back home."

June tried to ignore the knot forming in her stomach. "He sure doesn't act like it."

"It's still a big adjustment for him. Remember, before he moved to the retirement home, he lived here alone for twenty years. He's pretty set in his ways. It's not easy for a leopard to change his spots, as they say. He'll get used to us in time."

"I hope so." June couldn't help wondering. "He was so nice when he asked us to move in here with him. Now he's back to normal."

"He's just worn-out, that's all." Her mom smoothed down June's flyaway hair. "At seventy-three, you tire easily."

A sharp bang, followed by shattering glass, brought them both to their feet. June raced ahead of her mom into the kitchen. There stood Franklin, shoulders drooping. Shards of broken glass filled the sink.

"Are you all right?" June's mom asked.

Franklin nodded, suddenly looking beaten. "I'm sorry, Anne. I'll clean it up."

But June had already picked up the biggest pieces of glass and thrown them in the garbage. With a wet paper towel, she wiped out the remaining sparkling slivers.

Anne Finch poured three glasses of lemonade. "Come sit a minute. You, too, June." She placed the glasses on coasters so they wouldn't hurt the varnished dining-room table. "We've all worked so hard unpacking this afternoon. We need a break."

June collapsed gratefully at the table, but Franklin continued to poke around in the cupboard. Within seconds he'd scrambled the herbs and spices Anne had so neatly organized.

"Not here." Franklin slammed the door.

"Can I help you find something?" Anne asked.

"Time to take my medicine." Franklin pulled his black sweater closer around him. "*Somebody* hid it."

"No one hid it. It's in the bathroom," June's mom said. "But you only take it once a day."

"It's time *now.*"

June distinctly recalled watching Franklin take his heart medicine earlier. "You had it after breakfast, remember?" she asked, trying to be helpful.

"I didn't ask you!"

Ignoring the lemonade, he raked bony fingers through his white, wispy hair. June caught a glimpse of panic in his eyes before he stomped out of the room.

"I guess Doc Thompson was right when he said Franklin got mixed up about his medicine." June finished her lemonade, then drained Franklin's untouched glass. "Clara said the same thing last year when he was at the retirement ranch."

Her mom nodded. "It's only natural to be forgetful at his age. We'll just have to live with it." Smiling softly, she reached across the table and squeezed June's hand. "It's a small price to pay for living here and being home with you while I recover."

June searched her mom's lined face. It was still too thin to suit her. Suffering with ulcers had taken its toll.

Anne had been hospitalized with bleeding ulcers in the spring, and they'd sold their own small house to pay the enormous hospital bills. When packing to move to June's aunt's house in Cincinnati, Franklin had invited them to move into his old house on Brewster Street instead. June's mother was to be his companion and housekeeper, and make sure he took his medicine at regular times. Even with Franklin's unpredictable moods, it was easier work than she'd always done as a waitress.

"I *am* grateful to Franklin for letting us live here," June agreed, tinkling the ice in her glass. "But he should remember it's because of *you* that he got to move back home again," she added loyally.

Even though June had thought Reed's Retirement Ranch was a homey place, Franklin had never fit in there. Only after weeks of effort on June's part during the foster grandparent program had Franklin come out of his grouchy shell at all. June had been determined to win him over, and by the end of the school year, they'd become good friends.

"Remember when he first came to the hospital?" her mom asked.

June nodded. "Franklin *was* real good to me while you were sick." A loud bang came from the rear of the house. "Uh-oh."

"Now what?" her mom asked with a lopsided smile. She set her glass in the sink and headed down the hallway.

June held her icy glass against her damp forehead. If only she could curl up with her battered copy of *Little Women*, maybe under a shade tree in the backyard, and dream away the afternoon. Everything had happened so fast—selling their house, moving in with Franklin. She needed some time to adjust to it all.

Sighing, she dragged herself to her feet. Unfortunately, time was wasting.

In the living room, June sorted through books piled high on the lumpy couch. Her mom's book on diagnosing childhood illnesses looked odd next to Franklin's *Gardening for All Seasons*.

Maybe Franklin wouldn't mind if she read some of his gardening books, June thought. She'd always read a lot. It had helped pass the time when her mom had waitressed such long hours and she'd lived too far from her friends to see them much. That was one reason June was so excited about the move to Franklin's house. Now she lived a lot closer to some of her school friends.

"Won't they be surprised when school starts?" she whispered to herself.

Coming to her own pile of books, she leaned *Heidi* and *Black Beauty* next to Franklin's *Design with Nature* and *Picture Book of Perennials.*

Yes, things were looking up, June decided. It's about time, too, she thought. It seemed as if life had been one long struggle after another, ever since her dad died.

June cocked her head to one side. From the back of the house echoed Franklin's cranky voice. She sighed, recalling her mom's words about trying to accept Franklin's blunt ways.

Unwrapping the last book, June wadded up the old newspapers they'd used for padding. Aiming at a packing box, she tossed the balls across the room. Whether she threw them underhanded, overhanded, or from behind her back, she missed the box each time.

"Good thing I never wanted to play basketball," she muttered, picking up the balls of newspaper.

Pulling *Design with Nature* from the shelf, June padded barefoot down the hall to her room. She needed a break from the heat. Maybe after reading for a while in front of her tiny oscillating fan, she'd feel like unpacking again.

As she passed Franklin's dim bedroom, she noticed him standing—statuelike—in front of an old dressing table. His wistful expression was reflected in the huge round mirror attached to the table. He stared at something in his hand.

"Franklin?" June whispered. "Are you all right?"

He remained still for a moment, then slowly turned and blinked. "What?"

June stepped hesitantly into the darkened room. The pulled shades gave the illusion of coolness. "I asked if you were okay."

Franklin nodded slowly, then held out his hand. "This was Ella's." A faded, yellowed portrait of his wife, Ella, gazed at them from the dressing table.

June leaned close to peer at the locket Franklin held in his bent fingers. Heart-shaped, it had a tiny rose painted on the porcelain cover.

"Ooh, Franklin, that's beautiful. It was your wife's?"

He nodded slowly. "My wedding present to her." His gnarled fingers fumbled with the catch on the locket. Grunting in exasperation, he handed it to June. "Here. You open it."

June slid a thumbnail between the halves of the locket and popped it open. Inside, facing each other, were tiny photos of a much younger Franklin and a pretty girl. Both were unsmiling, but the girl's eyes twinkled under her curled bangs.

June studied the pictures. It was hard to see the Franklin she knew in this old photo, but the bushy eyebrows and hawklike nose were the same. Still, he'd been a handsome young man, June thought. She laid the locket beside the photo on the dressing table.

"It's really beautiful, Franklin. Ella must have treasured it." She lightly touched the rose on the cover. "I wish I had something like this, a place to keep tiny pictures of my folks. Then, when I really missed my dad, I could just open the locket and look at him."

Silently, Franklin stared at Ella's picture. Feeling as

if she had intruded on something private, June touched Franklin's arm, then turned and left his room.

No longer interested in reading, June left the book in her room and headed outdoors. Stepping out onto the creaking porch, June plopped down on the top step and leaned against the railing. She glanced across the street to where three small kids wrestled on the grass. Jenkins, they'd said their name was.

June leaned back and closed her eyes. She liked the neighborhood, especially living closer to her friends. But would she ever be comfortable inviting them over? She had to wonder. With Franklin so grouchy sometimes, he might scare off every friend she made.

Well, if it didn't work out, their arrangement wouldn't last forever. Her mom had only agreed to a six-month trial period of living together. Even so, June hoped with all her heart that they were here to stay.

Noting the wilted leaves of the potted geraniums on the steps, June took the watering can from the porch and filled it at the spigot on the side of the house. She loved caring for Franklin's plants. They softened the house's shabbiness, giving it a welcoming look.

June knew Franklin hoped their arrangement worked out, too. Otherwise he'd have to go back to Reed's Retirement Ranch. And June's mom looked forward to her new job as his housekeeper/companion, since it gave her much more time with June.

Most of all, June didn't want to move to Cincinnati, away from all her friends. Admittedly, one of those special friends was Franklin. He wasn't very good with words, but they'd grown to depend on each other during the past year. He was the only "grandfather" she'd ever known.

June stood and stretched, then turned to go back inside. She guessed they all had a lot at stake.

2
Getting in Tune

*J*une's panic over starting junior high the following Monday morning was temporarily forgotten in the relief of spotting a familiar face on the bus. When she climbed aboard the city bus at Fourth and Brewster, Sandy Hanes slid over to make room. June gratefully fell into the seat beside her, giggling as Sandy told one hilarious story after another.

As they stepped off the bus at Benjamin Franklin Junior High, however, her joy evaporated.

June dug in her purse for her class schedule. "I hope I can find my homeroom. What room do you have?" She turned toward Sandy, but her friend had already skipped halfway across the school yard.

"See you later, June!" Waving, Sandy shook her reddish orange hair comically, then joined Russell Mackey.

Dreamy in a navy blue sweater, he lounged on the school steps, tossing a football in the air and catching it.

June glanced around anxiously. Sandy obviously didn't want her company anymore. What was she supposed to do?

Slinging her duffel bag of gym clothes over her shoulder, she wandered down the sidewalk toward the old brick building. Deafening screeches filled the air as friends yelled to each other. Suddenly she felt shy about joining a group. With her mom needing constant care all summer, June hadn't seen anyone but Sandy since last spring.

Then she spotted Holly Nichols standing alone under a maple tree. Her long, frizzy black hair was pulled back with glittery plastic butterfly clips.

"Holly!" June called, her voice a mere squeak.

"Hi, June! Haven't seen you all summer."

"I know." June hurried toward her. "You'll never guess what happened."

As she came around the side of the tree, June halted at the sight of Jason White. Silent as a statue, he leaned against the tree trunk, his silver-framed sunglasses reflecting the morning glare.

"I'll never guess what?" Holly prompted her.

Feeling tongue-tied in front of the stony Jason, June stammered, "Oh, uh, well, I've moved."

"Where to?"

"Brewster and Fourth." She turned her back to Jason and lowered her voice. "Remember my foster grandfather from the project last year? Mom and I moved into his old house with him."

"No kidding! With that old grouch?"

"Um, yes, well, he's not so bad." June's voice trailed off. Although Jason never said a word, she got the feeling from his loud sighs that she'd interrupted something. "Well, I've got to go. See you."

Shaking her wispy blond bangs out of her eyes, June waved, then hurried off with big strides across the school yard as if she had somewhere important to go, someone to meet.

Inside, though, her stomach churned. Had all her friends paired off during the summer? Last year in elementary school, they'd all done things together in a big group. Now everyone was in groups of two. It was as if her friends had sailed ahead and left her behind during the summer.

Most of the groups she passed were older kids. A few boys from her last year's sixth-grade class were gathered around a fire plug, but June wasn't about to join *their* group. From what she could see, their main entertainment consisted of smacking each other with their duffel bags or karate chopping each other.

When the bell rang, June headed inside and up to the second floor to homeroom 201. Trying to keep her balance as she was knocked into a wall by students rushing to class, June thought she might consider weight lifting as her new hobby.

Around the corner, she poked her nose inside room 201. A handful of students milled around, but they were strangers to June. They must have come from other elementary schools in town.

"Psssst! June." From the back of the room, Suzy Atkins waved her long, manicured nails.

Flooded with relief, June moved down the aisle, trying not to hit anyone with her duffel bag. "Hi, Suzy. You look neat." June slid into the corner desk, admiring her friend's casual pose.

Suzy always looked as if she had stepped straight from the pages of a fashion magazine. Even if she could afford Suzy's outfit, June knew she'd never have the confidence to wear it. But that was Suzy, always starting new trends, from oversized army jackets one year to vests down to her knees, like the one she wore today.

Rolling her eyes, Suzy whispered, "Did you see our homeroom teacher? He's standing outside the door."

June craned her neck, but couldn't spot him. She'd been so busy hunting for the right room number that she hadn't looked at anybody's face.

Suzy smacked her lips. "Be prepared for a hunk. Just don't look into his baby blue eyes. You'll melt!"

"Thanks for the warning." June smiled nervously and smoothed her slacks, wondering if she should have dressed up more for the first day of school. Actually, since she wasn't wearing jeans, she thought she *was* dressed up.

"What'd you do to kill time this summer?" Suzy asked.

"Well, I . . ."

"I took that cheerleading workshop in June and July. I was great! You should have been there." Suzy leaned close to June's ear. "Just wait till tryouts for football cheerleader. It's in the bag."

18

June didn't doubt it. What Suzy wanted, Suzy got. If she wanted to be the junior-high principal badly enough, she could probably sweet-talk her way into *that* job.

"Whoo, whoo, Suzy-Q!"

Suzy whirled around to the desk on the opposite side. "Dave! Just the guy I wanted to see."

As usual, Dave Sandler's blond hair and extremely fair skin were accented by his bright pink cheeks. It didn't matter how nice the weather was. He always looked as if he'd come in out of subzero temperatures.

June leaned back with a sigh, trying not to care that Dave hadn't spoken to her. It wasn't that she liked him or anything—she wasn't too wild about boys at all—but it made her feel invisible.

The day dragged by. June liked most of her teachers and classes, but the confusion of moving from room to room made her head ache. Once she'd ended up in a ninth-grade sewing class instead of her math room. She'd just about died of humiliation.

Exhausted at 3:30, she hurried alone to her locker. She'd quit hunting for someone to walk around with. All her friends were as lost as she was. Grabbing her homework, June raced toward the bus stop.

"Hey, June, wait up!"

June turned to find Sandy running after her, her orange hair a fireball against the blue sky. "Where's Russell?" she asked when Sandy fell into step beside her.

"Football practice. Has it every day."

"Really?" June's spirits rose. "Then you'll be riding the bus every afternoon?"

"Yup." They climbed aboard and got their ticket passes punched. "Mind if I get off with you?"

"Why?"

"I just live two blocks from your stop. Maybe we could talk a while or something, then I'll head home." She snapped her fingers. "I know. I could walk to your stop every morning and get on with you, too."

"I'd like that." June grinned widely. Sandy wasn't going to be too busy for her after all.

The bouncy ride home was filled with Sandy's loud opinions of her new teachers. June didn't *really* think their English teacher, Mrs. Slingarten, looked like Adolf Hitler, but she pretended to agree. And she didn't *honestly* believe Sandy when she said the principal tossed tardy kids into cages in his office. But she'd agree to almost anything not to have to walk home alone after school again this year.

Wrinkled and sticky, they stepped off the bus ten minutes later. "Well, there it is." June pointed to Franklin's house.

"What was that old guy's name again?"

"Franklin Cooper. See the mailbox?" On the porch was the black mailbox she'd repainted. Underneath *F. Cooper* were neat red letters that said *A. and J. Finch.*

Just then June's mom and Franklin came out, carrying tall glasses. Slowly they eased into the porch swing, one of the few pieces of furniture June's mom had added to Franklin's house, since he didn't already have one.

"Well, see you in the morning," June said with a wave.

To her surprise, Sandy ignored her wave and strutted right up the sidewalk to the front porch. With a sense of dread, June followed slowly behind.

"Hi, Mrs. Finch!" Sandy called. "I haven't seen you in a long time."

"We'll have to do something about that, won't we?" Anne Finch slowly pushed the creaky swing with her foot. "Would you girls like some lemonade? Then you can tell us about your day."

At Franklin's scowl, June opened her mouth to say that Sandy had to get right home. However, her friend had already plopped down on the step. "Sounds great, Mrs. F. I nearly died of thirst on that bus."

June's mom laughed. "Here, take my glass then. I'll get some more. It's okay—I haven't touched it."

Sandy gulped gratefully as Anne Finch went inside. Franklin slumped in the swing and stared down his hawk-like nose at Sandy. Glancing up, Sandy squinted and stared right back.

Franklin pointed a bony finger at Sandy. "I know you."

"Yup. Probably from Reed's Retirement Ranch," Sandy agreed, slurping noisily. "I was in June's class when we visited all you old people."

Franklin rocked violently back in the swing, slopping his lemonade over the rim. June winced. Franklin hated being called one of the "old people."

June's heart hammered in her ears. "Um, I'm surprised you can remember Sandy, out of all those kids who visited last year."

"Not hard." Franklin snorted. "Only clowns have hair that color."

June gasped, but to her relief, Sandy just laughed and ran her fingers through her hair. "True enough!" She glanced at Franklin's white wispy fringe of hair over his ears. "At least it beats going bald, huh?"

Franklin's eyes bulged and his mouth opened and closed, but not a word came out. June leaned forward, terrified that his heart was beating too fast again. She hoped he'd taken his medicine on time that day.

Sandy leaned back against the porch railing and breathed deeply. "This looks like a nice, cozy little house," she said, turning to June. "That was nice of your mom to help out old Franklin here so he could move back home."

June glanced at Franklin's reddening face. "Well, actually . . ."

Franklin leaned forward in the swing. "It was nice of *me* to help *them* out, you mean. They had nowhere to go."

Sandy frowned. "I thought they were moving to Cincinnati."

"They didn't want to," Franklin argued. "They begged me to take them in, so I did."

June's mouth dropped open. That wasn't exactly the way it had happened!

Sandy frowned at June. "Wasn't your mom against the whole idea? I thought you had to convince her to give it a try."

Saliva gathered in the corners of Franklin's mouth.

It slowly ran down his chin, reminding June of a mad dog. "That's not how I remember it," he growled.

"Oh, don't worry about it," Sandy said, waving her arm airily. "At your age, memory loss is quite common. Why, I've got a great-grandma who can't even remember her own name. She insists that she's Queen Elizabeth."

Franklin's arm jerked, and his lemonade ran down his pants leg, but he barely noticed. June could hear his raspy breathing over the creaking of the swing. She wished she could magically sink beneath the porch floor.

When her mom came back, June heaved a sigh of relief. With only a quick glance at Franklin, she settled in the swing again. Soon she was chatting easily with Sandy about her classes and her family.

At 4:15 Sandy drained her glass. "Gotta scoot. Mom said to beat it home after school. Thanks for the lemonade."

June walked Sandy to the corner. When she got back Franklin had gone inside, so June took his place in the swing.

Her mom patted her knee. "Why the long face? Was it a rough day?"

"Not real bad." June glanced toward the screen door and lowered her voice. "But you should have heard Franklin while you were inside. He said Sandy's hair looked like it belonged on a clown."

"Oh, no."

"Isn't there some way to get Franklin to, you know, be a little friendlier? It's kind of embarrassing, the way he talks."

"I know he's blunt, but I don't think he means to be cruel. It's just his way. We might as well accept it. That's part of what makes Franklin *Franklin*."

June nodded. Her mom probably was right, but little by little, her dream of having a happy home where she could invite her friends was slipping away.

June's mom gave her a quick hug. "Would you like me to talk to him for you? Maybe I could do something to help."

June sighed. "I guess not." She swirled the melted ice in her glass. "I can handle it."

Her mom studied her thoughtfully. "You've sure grown up lately. Yes, I guess you can handle it just fine."

"I have a ton of homework," June said a few moments later, patting her duffel bag. "Maybe I can get some done now. I'll help you with supper in about an hour, if that's okay."

For months while her mom was sick, June had done *all* their cooking and cleaning, and even though things had changed, it still felt like her responsibility.

"No need, honey. It's in the oven already." She pulled June down for a quick kiss, then gave her a gentle push toward the front door. "Just hit the homework."

Inside, June was heading toward her bedroom when she heard a gravelly "harrumph." Peeking around the corner, she saw Franklin at one end of the long dining-room table. His checkers were set up for a game.

June held up her books. "I'm really sorry, Franklin. I have a test to study for."

His eyebrows drew together in a dark scowl.

June took a deep breath. During the past year when she'd visited Franklin at the retirement home, they'd played checkers nearly every week. It took months, but finally June had beaten him for the first time. It never happened often though.

"I really *do* have a lot of homework," June said weakly. She felt herself shrivel under Franklin's gaze. "Well, maybe one game won't take too long."

Franklin gazed slowly around the room. "It's the least you could do," he muttered.

June silently finished the sentence for him: "Because you're living in *my* house." Dragging her chair close, June tried to concentrate on jumping Franklin's red kings.

Her mom walked through the room ten minutes later. "I thought you had homework."

June smiled weakly. Her mom nodded knowingly before turning toward the kitchen. Abruptly, she whirled around. "I almost forgot to tell you!"

"Tell me what?"

"You know the upright piano in the living room? Remember how out of tune it was when we moved in?" Her eyes danced with excitement. "Franklin got it tuned today, and it sounds beautiful. Wait! I'll play something for you. I found several old songbooks in the bench."

June glanced at Franklin, her irritation at him melting away. Tuning the piano was a thoughtful thing for him to do. Her mom had played years ago, but they hadn't owned a piano of their own. She'd really enjoy playing Franklin's piano in her spare time.

Franklin caught her smile and scowled back. "Your turn."

June slid her checker forward, knowing Franklin was embarrassed by being caught doing a kind deed.

Her mom ran up and down a few scales, then called, "This is going to be 'The Rocky Glen Two Step.' I'm awfully rusty, so be patient!"

Soon the festive melody filled the tiny rooms as her mom's fingers raced up and down the keys. June was amazed how much better the piano sounded after having been tuned. And her mom sounded thrilled to be playing again after so many years.

June reached across and patted Franklin's rough hand. "Thanks for being so nice to Mom."

"Humph. Pay attention. Your turn," Franklin snapped.

Trying not to smile, June jumped one of Franklin's kings. The piano wasn't the only thing that needed tuning, she decided. She and Franklin were not exactly harmonious. June couldn't tell if *she* was out of tune, or if it was Franklin. She suspected it was Franklin. Either way, they sure clashed sometimes.

Too bad he wasn't an old piano, June thought dryly, because she didn't know anyone who did tune-ups on off-key people.

3
The Toothache Tree

*T*he first week of school passed in a blur as June learned where her classes were and did homework every night. By Friday afternoon's history class, she'd decided junior high was okay—except for one thing.

She couldn't deny it. Over the summer her friends had changed. Instead of moving in one big fun-loving group, they'd mostly separated into boy-girl pairs. Although she tried to ignore it, June felt out of step with Sandy, Holly, and Suzy. She had no boyfriend to walk her to class or sit by her at lunch.

She didn't even *want* one. To June, that was the real problem.

"Miss Freemont, please come to the office for a telephone call." With a scratchy squawk, the intercom fell silent.

June glanced up, her pencil poised above her worksheet on Aztec Indians. Miss Freemont, her braces gleaming, headed for the door.

"Juth finith your worktheet and drop it on my dethk when you leave," she lisped. "And have a good weekend."

Ten seconds after the door shut behind Miss Freemont, June was hit with a spit wad. As she wiped the slime from her arm, another spit wad whizzed by, this time splattering Whistler North, who sat in front of her. Trying to ignore the chaos, June finished describing what Aztec Indians used to eat.

When the bell rang, June slowly gathered her papers and books together. Being small, she'd already been knocked down twice that week, so she hung back until the stampede passed. She knew Sandy would wait for her at the bus stop anyway, so there was no use risking her life to be the first one out the door.

Anyway, Whistler's husky form blocked the aisle in front of her. Waiting for him to move, June studied the cowlick at the back of his head. Apparently it had been glued down at one time, but defiant chunks had broken loose to spring up.

"Um, excuse me," June finally said. The classroom was nearly empty, but Whistler's bulk still blocked her way.

"Sorry." Whistler sat back down to let her pass. "You're always so quiet, I forget you're back there."

June smiled. "That happens to me a lot," she said, moving down the aisle.

However, nobody *ever* forgot Whistler was in the

room. Even if he weren't the biggest kid in class, everyone would know he was there. He laughed constantly and joked with everybody, but June noticed he was alone a lot too, and never paired with a girl.

Just ahead of June, Jason White tossed his worksheet on the teacher's desk, then pulled his sunglasses from his pocket. Reaching around him, June added hers to the pile. With a smirk, Jason took a swipe at the papers on the desk, sending them flying across the floor, then slipped on his sunglasses and headed out the door.

"Outta my way," he snarled as he brushed by her.

Of all the nerve, June thought, watching Jason disappear down the hall.

At the sound of rustling paper, she glanced over her shoulder. Down on his hands and knees, Whistler huffed and puffed as he gathered up the scattered papers. Stacking them neatly on the desk again, he weighted them down with a potted cactus.

Hitching up his jeans, he spotted June watching him from the door. "Don't tell anyone you saw me cleaning up," he warned, turning pink at the ears. "I have a reputation to think of!"

June laughed. "Your secret's safe with me. If you do stuff like that, though, you'll end up being teacher's pet."

"A fate worse than death." Whistler made stabbing motions through his heart, then tucked his shirt in over his round stomach.

Watching him, June was amazed at the tiniest of flutters in her stomach. She'd actually enjoyed talking to a boy just then! Admittedly, with his cowlicks and freckles, Whistler was no movie star. Still, June found him a lot more likable than Jason White, who thought he was God's gift to junior-high girls.

"See you, Whistler," June said.

Whistler winked at her. "Remember—this is our secret." With a wave, he bounced off down the hall to be swallowed by the pushing crowd.

June sighed, then turned toward her locker. Whistler North was no handsome football captain like Russell, but he *was* awfully nice. Even pretty easy to talk to. Maybe . . . maybe he'd turn out to be somebody special.

June shook her head. Shoulders hunched, she zigzagged through the crowd. That kind of thing happened to other girls, not to her.

On Saturday morning June awoke to the sound of the back door slamming. Rolling over, she groaned at the numbers on her clock: 6:50 A.M. So much for sleeping in, she thought.

The door banged again, then again. The howling wind sounded cold for the middle of September. "Better go hook the door before the glass breaks," she mumbled.

Stumbling through the kitchen, June nearly tripped over a hoe left lying in the back entry. Beside it, the door was propped open by a watering can. With each gust of wind, the door flew open and banged closed on the can.

Puzzled, June peered out to the sunny backyard. The sugar maples were just beginning to turn orange, and the bronze and golden mums were in full bloom. At the back of the yard near the vacant lot, Franklin leaned on a spade.

June tiptoed back through the house and past her mom's closed door. Throwing on her most ragged jeans and sweatshirt, she went to join Franklin.

"What are you doing?" she called as she crossed the backyard, dragging the hoe.

Franklin jumped, then turned slowly. "Don't sneak up on me." He pointed to two open paper sacks. "Time to plant bulbs."

"In the fall?" June peered doubtfully at the lumpy flower bulbs. "They won't have time to bloom before winter."

Franklin snorted. "Of course not."

Sitting on the ground Indian-style, June waited quietly for an explanation, knowing her questions irritated Franklin. She wasn't in the mood to be called a "nosy young whippersnapper" so early in the morning.

Finally, Franklin continued. "You plant bulbs in the fall. Bulbs need a good winter freeze before blooming in the spring." He measured off a rectangular shape. "The Dutch Master daffodils will go here, and the Raspberry Frills irises over there."

"Raspberry Frills?"

"They're purple and ruffled."

Five minutes later Franklin began to wheeze and had to stop. June took the spade and removed the rest of the sod. "Where should I put this grass?" she asked.

"Vacant lot." With the hoe, Franklin loosened the dirt in the new flower bed.

After dumping the sod in the vacant lot, June leaned on the spade and rubbed her forehead.

Franklin peered at her from under his bushy black eyebrows. "Something wrong with you?"

"Just a little headache. Guess I need to eat something."

Franklin crooked a bony finger, motioning for her to follow him. He hobbled to the vacant lot and stopped at a scraggly old tree. Snapping off several small twigs, he gave them to June.

"What'd you do that for?" she asked.

Franklin cleared his throat. "For toothaches, Indians used to chew the berries and twigs of the prickly ash tree. They called it the Toothache Tree."

June bit on one twig. "I'd think chewing a tree would make your toothache *worse.*"

"People take aspirin for a toothache or headache. The chemical in aspirin is also found in the berries and bark of this Toothache Tree."

June grinned. Just when she thought Franklin had lost his marbles, he surprised her with the neatest nature details.

"Hey, you two, breakfast!" Anne Finch called out the back door.

After eggs and muffins, they went back outside. June loved digging in the dirt with Franklin. Their love of wildflowers had brought them closer together last year at the retirement ranch. She still had the wild potato plant he'd given her on her birthday. When they'd decided to move in together, June had often dreamed of planting a garden with Franklin, just the two of them working side by side.

They hoed and planted silently for another hour, finishing the iris bed and starting on the daffodils. As the temperature climbed, June shed her sweatshirt.

"Franklin! Time for your medicine," June's mom called out the kitchen window.

Franklin continued to dig.

"Franklin!"

Franklin turned slowly. "I'm busy!"

"You come get it, or I'll come out there."

June grinned. "You might as well go in. You know she means business."

"Humph." Wheezing slightly, Franklin brushed the dirt from his black pants. "Bossy woman."

June placed more Dutch Master daffodil bulbs in the ground. "I can finish up," she said, wiping her muddy hands on her jeans. "Maybe you should rest."

Franklin scowled at her, then hobbled toward the house. "Bossy as your mother," he muttered.

Humming softly, June finished placing the flower bulbs, then began to cover them. According to her watch it wasn't even 11:00, but she was already starved for lunch.

June was watering the finished flower beds when the back door slammed again. As she watched in surprise, her mom streaked across the backyard toward her. A basket of wet laundry banged against her hip.

"What's wrong, Mom?"

"Nothing." Anne Finch smiled knowingly. "You have a caller."

"Who? Sandy?" June wiped her sleeve across her sweaty nose.

"A boy named Myron." At June's puzzled expression, her mom added, "Myron North?"

June's eyes opened wide. "You must mean Whistler North! I never knew his first name was Myron." She started to giggle, then her hand flew to her mouth. "Where is he?"

"In the living room, talking with Franklin."

"Oh, no."

June raced to the house and stepped inside the back entry, careful not to slam the door. Glancing in the hall mirror, she winced at the streaks of mud across her chin and cheeks. She'd have to clean up before rescuing Whistler.

June tiptoed to the bathroom for a wet washcloth, then stuck her head around the door to listen. She almost wished she hadn't.

"Folks call you Whistler?" Franklin's voice sounded accusing. "What's wrong with your real name?"

Whistler coughed a couple times. "I just like Whistler better, I guess. Sir."

"Then I guess you live with Whistler's mother." Franklin's cackling laugh soon turned into a loud rasping wheeze.

"Are you all right, Sir?"

"I'm fine," Franklin snapped when he could catch his breath.

June scrubbed frantically at her face, leaving it red and blotchy. She'd better get out there *fast*, just as soon as she changed her muddy clothes.

She strained to hear Franklin's next words. If only her mom would leave the wet laundry and hurry back inside to talk to Whistler. At this rate he'd never come to see her again.

"You play football?" Franklin asked abruptly.

"No, Sir."

"You should, hefty as you are."

June cringed, imagining Whistler's embarrassment. Slipping across to her bedroom, she changed into clean clothes, then hurried down the hall. She was ready to enter the living room when Franklin's words stopped her.

"You know June lives with me now?"

"Yes, Sir."

"Good."

June held her breath. What did Franklin mean by that?

Franklin's rocking chair creaked back and forth. "That makes me responsible for June, so I want to know something."

"Um, sure. What?"

"What are your intentions toward her?"

"My intentions?"

The creaking stopped abruptly. "I won't have anyone toying with her affections."

June's hands flew to cover her flaming cheeks. How could Franklin *say* such a thing? She wanted to die on the spot. Franklin was acting as if Whistler had come over to *marry* her instead of just to talk.

Whistler cleared his throat half a dozen times. "Gee, Mr. Cooper, I wouldn't toy with—whatever you just said. June's just a friend."

Wishing she could disappear, June took a deep breath and slinked into the living room instead. "Hi, Whistler."

Whistler's chair scraped backward as he stood. "Hi, June." He held up his social studies book. "Um, I just had a question about Miss Freemont's assignment."

"I'll get my book. I did the assignment last night."

"Well, actually, I was just on my way to the . . . um, the dentist, and it's almost time for my appointment." He made an elaborate show of studying his wristwatch. "In fact, if I don't leave right away, I'll be late."

Her mind a total blank, June watched Whistler back toward the door.

"Well, be seeing you at school, June. Bye, Mr. Cooper." After crashing into the door, he pivoted on his heel, flung the door open and was gone.

June wanted to melt right into the floor.

Eyebrows knit together, Franklin stared out the front window. "Nervous kid," he muttered.

June pressed her lips together and ran to her room. She was too embarrassed even to cry, but her head really throbbed now. She ought to run outside to the vacant lot for a super dose from the Toothache Tree.

Throwing herself face down across her bed, June wished she could find a Heartache Tree instead.

4

Nobody's Perfect

❦❧❦

*T*hat afternoon June helped her mom take the dry
laundry from the clothesline. She was still embarrassed about Franklin's treatment of Whistler. He'd
humiliated the only boy who'd ever come to see her.
How would she ever face Whistler on Monday?

June lay the folded terry bath towel in the basket.
"Living with Franklin isn't like I planned at all."

"That's why I insisted on a six-month trial period,
in case things don't work out like we hoped. Try not to
take his remarks personally though."

June grabbed a handful of clothespins. "If Franklin really liked me, how could he embarrass me that
way?"

"Oh, honey, he does like you. A lot more than you
think." Anne Finch put her arm around her daughter's

shoulders. "Why do you suppose Franklin asked Whistler about his reasons for coming to see you?"

June thought back to the painful conversation. "He said since I lived under his roof, he was responsible for me. Like he owned me or something."

"Maybe Franklin just felt protective and wanted to make sure you had nice friends—kids who would treat you well." June's mom leaned against the clothesline pole, breathing hard. "I remember your dad being the same way. When you were a baby, I used to feel a bit hemmed in at home, and wanted to go back to school. But your dad said no—that I'd work myself sick, studying and trying to take care of you, too." Shading her eyes, June's mom peered thoughtfully at the fleecy clouds overhead. "At first, I resented what he said, but I came to realize it was his way of showing concern for me." She nodded toward the house. "I bet those are Franklin's feelings too."

June nudged the laundry basket with her toe. "Maybe . . ."

For another five minutes, they silently folded towels and pillowcases. It had been a perfect day to hang out wash, but a brisk wind had sprung up, and clouds hid the sun. Shivering, June pulled her sweater close around her.

As they folded the last sheet, Anne Finch lay a gentle hand on June's arm. "Do try to accept Franklin's behavior if you can. I know it's difficult, but he has a right to be himself." She glanced at the empty windows. "Remember—it's *his* house. We owe so much to him. Let's not forget that."

June sighed. "Do you think it'll take him a long time to get used to us?" She balanced the basket of clothes on her hip.

"Franklin will get used to us before long, but he may never change," Anne Finch said. "Franklin deserves to be accepted as a human being—with both his good points and his faults. We all need that. But it doesn't mean he'll change."

"I *do* like Franklin." June lowered her voice as they reached the back step. "Still, it wouldn't hurt him to change just a little."

Her mom grinned. "I know, but just try to concentrate on his better points."

Holding the door open, June knew her mom just didn't understand. June had her heart set on a fun home where she could invite her friends. Instead, Franklin's blunt ways drove them away.

If only her mom were stronger. Then June could go visit her friends—especially those nearby like Sandy—at their houses. But with her mom still so frail, she needed June's help after school and on weekends.

June sighed as she put away the folded laundry. In many ways, her life hadn't changed much at all.

On Sunday it drizzled while June spent the afternoon curled up on the couch with a book. Across the room, her mom softly practiced an old piece of music called "Rockaway." June enjoyed listening to her and wished the day would last forever.

Anything to avoid seeing Whistler at school the next day.

But on Monday morning she was dismayed to come down the corridor and find Whistler waiting near her locker. Heart pounding, June drew back around the corner. At the sight of him, the apology she'd so carefully rehearsed evaporated into thin air.

Trying to look casual, June rummaged through her notebooks as if hunting for something. A minute later she peeked around the corner. Whistler wasn't gone yet, but he wasn't leaning against her locker anymore.

June watched as he joked with Miss Freemont at the water fountain. Arms full of golden chrysanthemums, the teacher was filling two vases with water. When the containers were filled, Miss Freemont turned, still laughing at something Whistler had said, and entered her classroom. She was jostled by two boys, and some of the water slopped out.

The halls slowly emptied, but June watched Whistler in amusement. After looking up and down the nearly deserted halls, he whipped out his handkerchief and hurriedly mopped up the puddle. In thirty seconds, he had stuffed the handkerchief back in his pocket and was leaning against June's locker once again.

Smiling, June came around the corner. "I saw you doing more good deeds," she whispered.

A pink flush crept up Whistler's neck. "I just didn't want anybody to slip and fall." He cleared his throat several times. "June, about rushing off Saturday . . ."

June twirled her padlock combination, then pulled her math and science books out. "Did you have any cavities?" she asked.

"Huh?" Whistler blinked. The pink flush spread to his neck and cheeks. "Oh. My dentist appointment. No, no cavities."

Suddenly the memory of Whistler crashing out their front door struck her funny. June tried to strangle the giggle rising inside her, but it escaped anyway.

"I'm sorry, Whistler. Saturday wasn't funny at all."

Whistler grinned sheepishly. "I guess you know there wasn't a dentist appointment."

"I figured that."

"Sorry I ran out. I only wanted some help with the social studies paper." He thumped his untied tennis shoe against the green locker. "I wasn't ready for that old guy to ask my . . . my . . ."

"Intentions."

"Yeah, intentions toward you."

"It's okay. That's just Franklin's way. He doesn't mean anything by it," June said, surprised to hear herself echoing her mom's words. She slammed her locker and moved away toward homeroom. "See you later."

After school June picked cooked chicken off the bones while she watched her mom stir eggs and flour together for homemade noodles.

She'd left Franklin in the porch swing a minute ago, "resting his eyes," as he called it. When June asked why closing his eyes always made him snore, he'd only grunted and scowled at her.

Clearing the countertop to make room to roll out

the noodles, June's mom picked up a green slip of paper. "What's this?"

"Nothing." June wiped her greasy fingers on a paper towel. "I meant to throw that away when I cleaned out my bag."

"The note says your class is having a Father-Daughter Banquet early in November. Wouldn't you like to go?"

June concentrated on picking the meat off a drumstick. "I don't have a father to take."

"I know. But it also says you can invite a grandfather if you have one living nearby."

Her statement sounded more like a question, but June refused to meet her mother's eyes, pretending she didn't understand. She *couldn't* take Franklin. She just couldn't.

"June?"

June played with a greasy chicken bone while her stomach twisted into a knot. "I know what you're thinking, but I can't invite him." Her voice was barely more than a whisper. "I'd never survive a whole meal in public with Franklin."

"Would it really be so bad?"

Guilt washed over June as she tried to explain. "We'd have to eat at little tables and make conversation with strangers. You *know* how he talks. He'd probably say 'this meat's tough as shoe leather,' or the glee club singers 'can't carry a tune in a bushel basket.' I'd just die!"

"It's okay. I understand." Anne Finch sliced the noodles into long strips to dry. "Anyway, Franklin won't ever know about the banquet, so there's no chance of hurting his feelings. I just hate to see *you* miss it."

"Believe me, this is one event I don't mind missing at all." June smiled to soften her words.

After homemade chicken and noodles for supper, which Franklin pronounced fit for a king, the three of them washed the dishes together. It had become a nightly ritual June looked forward to. For years, she'd done the dishes alone while her mom worked or rested, so she loved having the company. She and her mom could probably finish in half the time if Franklin didn't help, but it was one time of day he was usually in a good mood. Tasty food seemed to soften his rough edges.

Anne dried the last plate and handed it to Franklin to put away. June rinsed out the sink and wiped her hands on a towel.

"Up to a game?" Franklin challenged June. "Or are you afraid I'll thrash you again?"

"Me, afraid? No way. You just got lucky last time." June bowed at the waist. "After you, Sir."

"Wait a minute, you two." June's mom licked her lips nervously. "I have something to show you."

She opened a small magazine, and June saw a list of adult education classes being offered later that fall. "Did you sign up for something, Mom?"

"No, at least not yet. I wanted to ask you both about it first." She pointed to the bottom of the first column.

June read aloud. " 'Learn touch typing skills. Essential for today's secretary. Introduction to word processing during final weeks of the course.' "

"What do you think?"

June was surprised, but it made sense. "A typing course sounds great. The classes are free, aren't they?"

"Yes, and I can ride the bus over to the high school where they're held. The classes meet on Tuesday and Thursday evenings." She leaned against the sink. "Then, when I got my strength back and could find a job, I wouldn't have to waitress. I could be a secretary. At least I could try."

Franklin poked the ad with his bony finger. "You'd be gone two nights every week?"

"You wouldn't be alone. June would be here."

Franklin shuffled toward the dining room. "No classes. No." Checkers rattled as he dumped them on the dining-room table.

June stood with her mouth hanging open. She watched in surprise as her mom folded the catalog and tossed it in the garbage. "Don't give up, Mom! I bet you could convince Franklin if you tried."

Her mom untied the apron from around her slender waist. "He doesn't feel comfortable with my being gone at night."

June fished the catalog out of the garbage and held it out toward her mom. "Don't let him keep you from this if it's something you really want."

"That's okay. Really. In fact, it's almost nice to feel needed again. You're growing up and need me less and less. I miss that—your needing me. If we had to move to Cincinnati, *no one* would need me there. Sharon has Bill, and you'd make new friends." She gestured around the warm kitchen. "At least here Franklin needs me. My presence is really important to him."

June cocked her head to one side. This was a new

side of her mom. "But I *do* need you," she protested. In fact, June couldn't imagine what she'd do without her mom!

"I know." Her mom hugged her close, then lowered her voice. "Besides, there's another reason I should be here. Franklin's had a couple of spells while you were at school. I think they scared him."

"What kind of spells? His heart?"

"More like anxiety attacks, Doctor Thompson said. But Franklin thinks it's his heart. He might be afraid to be alone at night, even with you for company, in case of an emergency."

June admitted to herself that she wasn't too wild about the idea either. "If it's not his heart, though, I could keep an eye on him." She wrapped her arms around her mom's tiny frame. "Don't give up on the typing classes," she whispered. "Not yct."

Her mom's smile was tired and lopsided. "It's okay. Maybe I could borrow a typing book from the library and learn, if I ever save enough money for a secondhand typewriter. For now, though, I'd better put it on hold. We do owe Franklin a lot, remember."

June shook her head. She wished her mom wouldn't give up on the night classes. A secretary's job would be so much better than a waitressing job—less exhausting, more money, and better hours. They did owe Franklin a lot, June knew, and she was grateful. Yet they had to think of the future, too.

However, it wasn't June who came up with a solution to the problem. It was Sandy.

The next day after school Sandy stood talking on the sidewalk in front of Franklin's house. Her conversation consisted mostly of "Russell this" and "Russell that," but June didn't mind. She'd gladly listen to stories of "Russell the Magnificent," just to have Sandy's company.

As they talked, strains of "Scarborough Fair" floated out the open window. "Does your mom play the piano?" Sandy asked.

"No, it's Franklin." June tried to keep a straight face at the thought, but couldn't. "Yes, it's my mom."

"She's good." Sandy closed her eyes and swayed back and forth on the sidewalk, waltzing with an imaginary Prince Charming. Suddenly she threw down her books and grabbed June's arm. "May I have this dance?"

"Sandy! Stop it!" June giggled as Sandy waltzed her around and around on the sidewalk. June tried to keep up, but soon her feet and Sandy's tangled, and they collapsed dizzily in a heap on the grass.

Panting, Sandy fanned her red face and hummed along with the rest of the song. "Does your mom give lessons? She should."

"No, she just plays for herself and Franklin." June snapped her fingers. "That's it!" She scrambled to her feet, waved to Sandy and raced up her sidewalk. "Thanks for the great idea!"

She burst into the living room, letting the screen door bang. Her mom whirled around on the piano bench. "Where's the fire?"

Taking several deep breaths, June tried to speak

slowly. "There's one way you can earn money and still not wait tables anymore. You wouldn't have to leave Franklin all alone either. You could even earn money right away."

"You've lost me."

"Sandy heard you playing and asked if you gave piano lessons. How about it?"

Her mom stared blankly at June. "Oh, I couldn't."

"Why not? You're good enough."

"I just couldn't. I only play for fun. I'm not that good. Anyway, working for Franklin should be enough for me."

June laughed and shook her finger at her mom. "You know, Mom, it's not a *crime* to get paid for doing something you'd really enjoy." Her smile faded. "Does life always have to be a struggle?"

Blinking in surprise, Anne Finch turned and ran her fingers lightly up and down the keyboard, hitting each ivory key, plus all the sharps and flats in between. When she turned, her eyes shone.

"*Maybe* I could! I'd never considered it." Then a shadow crossed her face. "But what would I do with Franklin during lessons? He won't always work outside like today," she whispered. "Can you imagine what he'd say to the students?"

"True."

Frowning, June stared at the piano keys. How could she have forgotten? Franklin was just like one of the black keys on the piano, she thought. Always dressed in black, and his tongue was definitely sharp.

June tossed her duffel bag on the chair and perched on the bench beside her mom. "When you have students, I could take Franklin for a walk . . . or play checkers in the back bedroom . . . or work in the flower gardens with him." June giggled quietly. "Or bind and gag him in the closet. Whatever works."

"June!"

"Just kidding. Just kidding." She patted her mom's hand, filled with warmth at the light in her mother's eyes.

By the first week in October, after advertising in the "job wanted" column of the local paper, her mom had five piano students. Most were beginners, and she seemed eager to start teaching them. June was proud of her mom for trying something new.

Now, if only Franklin could be kept on his best behavior during lesson times. June shook her head. It would take some fancy footwork to accomplish *that*.

5

Out of Tune

❀❀❀

"N ervous?" June asked her mom the following Saturday afternoon.

"No, not really."

Her mom polished the already sparkling piano keys, then adjusted the two piano books above the keyboard and centered the small clock on top of the piano. After sliding the piano bench half an inch backward, she moved it forward an inch.

"There, that's better." Anne Finch glanced up at June and grinned sheepishly. "Okay, I guess I *am* nervous. Just a little."

Perching on the edge of the bench, June put her arm around her mom's narrow shoulders. "You'll be great. Who's your first student?"

"A little first grader named Curtis Lyons." She patted

the pink piano books entitled *Piano Primer* and *Performance Primer*. "We'll start with these beginner books."

June pointed to the clock. "I'll see if Franklin's ready to go. We're walking down to the hardware store for an extra rake so we can clean up the leaves in the yard."

"That should keep him occupied long enough." She patted June's hand. "Thanks, honey."

Just then a brown station wagon pulled up out front. Anne hurried to the window. "He's here," she barely breathed. "How do I look?"

"Just great, Mom. Really." June peeked out the window to watch a skinny boy with curly hair scramble over five bodies to get out of the car. "I'll coax Franklin out the back way."

She and Franklin slipped out the kitchen door as she heard her mom say, "You must be Curtis. Won't you come in?" June said a quick prayer that things would go perfectly.

A blustery wind blew, and June hunched down inside her coat collar. Franklin, as usual, was bundled up in his black coat and black hat. In spite of the dark, overcast sky, his hat brim was pulled low, leaving his eyes lost in the shadows.

"Do we burn the leaves after we rake them? Or do we bag them for the garbage man?" June asked. "At our other house, we let the dead leaves decay on the lawn."

"Neither one."

"But if we don't do anything, won't the piles of leaves blow all over the yard again?"

Under his bushy black brows, Franklin rolled his

eyes. "Of course they'd blow around," he said with a snort. "We'll make compost."

"Compost? What's that?"

"Natural fertilizer—helps plants grow."

"You can turn leaves into fertilizer?" June asked doubtfully.

Franklin stomped across the yard. "You mix organic material, like these leaves, with some dirt, then let it decay. After a long time, it makes a natural plant fertilizer. Works better than all those new-fangled chemicals in the garden store."

A voice calling out from the house on the opposite corner interrupted them. "Hey, June, look!"

June waved at the little kids across the street. The Jenkins family had three kids, all younger than five. Most days they played outside, racing their Hot Wheels on the sidewalk, or studying ant hills, or shooting each other with sticks. Today they'd raked a pile of crunchy leaves and were taking turns jumping in it. June laughed as the kids crossed the street toward them on their way to town.

Squealing, the toddler waddled over to the leaf pile and tumbled facedown in it. Before he could roll out of the way, the four-year-old girl leaped through the air to land on top of him. The toddler's screams pierced the air.

June hurried to pick him up. She patted his back and wiped his tears, but he kept wailing. "There, there, you're all right." She picked bits of crushed leaves from his bibbed coveralls. Holding him close, June felt a rush of warmth and wished the kids' mom would ask her to babysit sometime.

As his sobs subsided, the front door flew open. June glanced up, expecting to see Mrs. Jenkins. Instead, a plump woman with rosy cheeks and white hair bounced across the lawn.

"Is Jimmy hurt?" She scooped him up in her ample arms. "Is my little Jimmy-kins all right? Let Gramma see the ouchie." She smothered his arm with kisses until his whimpers turned to giggles. "There, now. Gramma's little poochie-poo's all better. Who's your pretty friend, Jimmy?"

"I'm June Finch," she said, stifling a giggle. "I moved in across the street last summer."

The woman held out her plump hand, covered with sparkly rings. "I'm Maybelle Jenkins, the children's grandmother." She put little Jimmy down. A whiff of perfume that floated from the hankie tucked in her neckline was nearly overpowering. "I'm here to visit."

Maybelle turned, and her eyes opened wide as she spotted Franklin. He had remained on the sidewalk, silent. Maybelle bounced over to Franklin on her ridiculously small feet, then lay her plump hand on his sleeve. "I'm Maybelle Jenkins. And who might *you* be?"

Franklin stiffened and glared at her.

Maybelle dimpled and batted her eyelashes. "Don't tell me. I know! You're little Juney's daddy."

June's mouth fell open in surprise. Franklin—young enough to be her *father?* Oh, brother. Who would ever fall for that kind of flattery? She'd never seen an old lady flirt. Certainly nobody at Reed's Retirement Ranch had treated Franklin that way.

His voice was gravelly. "I'm Franklin Cooper. June's . . . er, grandfather."

Maybelle fairly danced in her tiny beaded slippers. "*Charmed,* I'm sure." She slipped her plump arm through his. "I see you're out for a breath of fresh air. I know— I'll come with you! I need someone to show me the sights."

Franklin glared down his long nose at her. "We don't have any sights."

"Oooh, Franklin, you're teasing little old Maybelle," she said, producing a lacey fan from her voluminous pocket. Snapping open the fan, she held it in front of her face and fluttered her eyelashes. June struggled to conceal her amazement.

Franklin backed up, stumbled over a tricycle on the sidewalk, and caught himself, all without taking his piercing eyes off Maybelle. "June!" he barked.

Waving to the kids, June hurried across the yard. "Nice to meet you, Mrs. Jenkins."

"Just call me Maybelle. Good friends shouldn't stand on ceremony." Her voice tinkled like wind chimes.

"Okay, Maybelle. Well, we'd better be going."

Without a word, Franklin marched back across the street to his house. June ran along beside him, plucking at his sleeve.

"Where are you going? We didn't get our rake yet."

Wheezing slightly, Franklin continued up the sidewalk to his front porch, muttering all the way. "Can't go outside . . . attacked by some ninny . . . old fool woman."

"Wait a minute! We still need the rake, don't we?"

Franklin ignored her. Panicking, June heard the young piano student still playing inside. How could she keep the promise to her mom now? It would take a miracle. Maybe Franklin wouldn't notice if she threw herself across the front door and barricaded him outside, she thought desperately.

Instead, she entered the living room on Franklin's heels. As she closed the door, she saw the old brown station wagon pulling up to the curb to pick up Curtis.

Inside, the little boy was perched at the piano. June noted with relief that only five minutes of his lesson were left. They'd been at the Jenkins house longer than she'd thought. In spite of Anne Finch's arm placed gently on his back, Curtis fidgeted back and forth.

"All right, Curtis, one more time." June's mom pointed to the beginning of a song called "The Balloon Man." "Sit still. We're almost done."

Hitting just two keys, Curtis pounded quarter notes over and over and over again. After only two measures, he was sliding back and forth again on the slick bench.

Franklin shuffled over and stood directly behind Curtis. When he pounded out the last note, Franklin spoke. "You have ants in your pants, kid?" he asked.

Curtis jumped off the piano bench about a foot. Whirling around, he stared wide-eyed at Franklin's scowling face. Slowly his lower lip began to quiver, then he jumped down and bolted for the front door.

June scrambled to block his exit. As Curtis threw the door open, June grabbed him from behind. Her fingers dug into his shoulders.

"Hey! Let go! You're hurting me!"

"Sorry." June pushed him back toward the piano, patting his sore arm. "You don't want to forget your piano books." Then, hooking her arm through Franklin's, she led him to the dining room. "Come on. Let's play checkers."

To her surprise, Franklin followed without protest. Glancing sideways, she noticed his startled expression. Evidently he'd also been surprised by Curtis's drastic reaction.

Ten minutes later, after a silent checker game, Franklin hobbled stiffly outside, mumbling something about watering the iris and daffodil bulbs. During their checker game, June had heard Curtis leave, but wondered if he'd be back. Weighed down with guilt at not keeping her promise, she went into the living room.

Anne Finch sat slumped at the piano, leaning on the closed lid.

"Mom?" Head hanging down, June's voice was barely more than a whisper. "I'm sorry I couldn't keep Franklin outside long enough."

Her mom straightened, then moved to the padded rocker. "It's okay. Thanks for catching Curtis before he escaped. At least he agreed to come back next week."

June sat at her feet, Indian-style. "How can Franklin act that way? He's going to drive away your piano students, plus my friends."

"I don't think he intends to," her mom said, rocking slowly. "I guess I'll have to do what I always tell you to do—accept him the way he is." She ran her fingers through her softly curled hair.

"Do you think he'll ever change?"

"I don't know." Anne gazed absentmindedly out the window, as if staring back in time. "I do know one thing, though, from living with your father. No one likes to feel pressured to change, to be different." A small smile played at the corners of her mouth. "I wish I'd learned that lesson sooner. It would have saved me lots of problems with your dad. I nagged him to change in many ways—mostly little things, some big ones—but it never did work. It might seem odd, but only when you accept someone *just the way he is* do you free him to change."

June didn't say anything, but she had a hard time grasping that. If they just accepted Franklin's behavior, he'd never change. Her mom's advice sounded kind of backward. How could accepting someone's embarrassing behavior inspire him to change?

June leaned against the rocker. She'd have to think about that for a long time before it made sense.

Supper was quiet that night. Most evenings, after some prompting, Franklin told funny stories about the people he'd known at Reed's Retirement Ranch. But that night he ate his tuna casserole with his head bent, staring at his plate.

Finally he put his fork down. "Anne, about this afternoon." He cleared his throat several times. "I didn't mean to upset the boy."

"I know. You just surprised him a little." Anne reached over and patted Franklin's arm. "He didn't know you were standing right behind him."

Just then June heard steps padding across their front porch, followed by a soft knock on the screen door. "Yoo-hoo! Oh, Franklin!"

Franklin's head jerked up in alarm.

"Who in the world?" June's mom asked.

June peeked through a slit in the curtain. "It's that lady from across the street, Mrs. Jenkins." She glanced at Franklin. "I mean, *Maybelle*."

"*Yoo-hoo!* Anybody home?"

June hurried to the living room and held the screen door open. "Come in, Maybelle. Mmm, that makes my mouth water."

Maybelle carefully held a pie in front of her. June couldn't tell what kind it was, but it was topped with four inches of golden-brown meringue.

"After you left today, I got to thinking that maybe you'd all like a pie." Maybelle tiptoed to the doorway leading to the dining room. "Oh, *there* you are!" She bounced over to Franklin, shaking the creaky floorboards as she went. "My own Henry, God rest his soul, used to love my lemon meringue." With a jangling of bracelets, she placed the pie in front of Franklin.

He scowled at the pie. His bony fingers plucked nervously at his shirt front.

"I'm sure we'll enjoy the pie," June's mom said. "That was very thoughtful. By the way, I'm Anne Finch."

"Well, howdy do! Glad to meet you." Maybelle pulled

out the fourth chair and plopped down. "Whew! Think I'll take a load off my feet, if you don't mind." She winked at Franklin.

June's lips twitched as Franklin sniffed the pie. "Doesn't smell like lemon. Smells like roses." He scowled. "None too fresh either."

Maybelle's laughter pealed like church bells. "Oh, my! Couldn't pull the wool over your eyes, I bet!" She leaned closer to Franklin and pulled the lacy hankie from her neckline. Waving it in front of his nose, she said, "This is what you smell. My Roses by Candlelight perfume."

"Smells lovely." Anne's nose wrinkled. "I can smell it way over here."

"Thank you!" Maybelle reached for Franklin's clean knife and sliced into the pie. "Here, let me get you some." She cut the pie into five generous pieces. Then, leaning close to Franklin, she slid a piece onto his plate.

His arms hanging down by his sides, he silently stared down at his plate, as if he'd never seen a pie in his life and had no idea what to do with it.

Maybelle nudged his arm. "Go ahead. Try it!" She bounced from one foot to the other, shaking the cut glass dishes in the old cupboard behind her. Franklin sat motionless. "Here, let me help you." Maybelle scooped up a huge forkful of meringue and waved it in front of his face. She got too close. A white blob of meringue was left sticking to the tip of Franklin's nose.

Anne jumped up, exclaiming loudly how good the pie looked. "Won't you stay and have a piece with us?"

Maybelle tossed her head, making her white curls

dance. "I can't. I'm babysitting for my daughter tonight and have to get right back. I didn't want to bother you folks. I just wanted to invite Franklin over tomorrow. My daughter-in-law needs two more people to fill in at her bridge club. I thought Franklin and I could help her out."

Franklin snorted, either from disgust or meringue in his nose. June couldn't be sure. "I don't play bridge," he said.

"Oh." Maybelle glanced around the room, her eyes lighting up at the checkerboard in the corner. "I see checkers is more your style. Mine, too." Sliding closer, she whispered coyly, "I always did like games for just two people. Who wants a crowd?"

At Franklin's horrified look, June giggled, nearly spewing out her milk. Franklin glared at her, and she stifled the giggle immediately.

Anne jumped up and slipped smoothly between Franklin and Maybelle. "Thanks again *so much* for the pie, Maybelle. We don't want to keep you from your babysitting job, though." Taking the plump lady's arm, she led her from the dining room. "Those active grandchildren must really keep you on your toes. . . ."

While her mom escorted Maybelle to the door, June stole a glance at Franklin's red face. Maybe she shouldn't feel sorry for him, but she couldn't help it. She hated to see Franklin so embarrassed, even though he was the cause of plenty himself.

But on the other hand, who knows? June thought. If Franklin's going to change, Maybelle might be just what the doctor ordered.

6

On Their Own

❦ ❦ ❦

*M*om, come quick! It's Uncle Bill." June covered the receiver. "Aunt Sharon had emergency surgery," she whispered, handing the phone to her mother.

Aunt Sharon was her mom's sister in Cincinnati. They'd almost moved in with her before school started. June remembered her roly-poly aunt visiting her mom in the hospital and how much it had cheered her up.

Breathing rapidly, June's mom took the phone. "Bill? How's Sharon? Is she all right?" She listened for a minute, her face sober. "Do the doctors expect complications?"

June slipped her arm around her mother's waist, wishing there were something she could do to help. Her mom loved Aunt Sharon; they were more like best friends than sisters. June thought having a sister must be one of the nicest things in the world.

June carried a chair to the phone so Anne could sit down, and her mother smiled gratefully. "Of course I'll come, Bill. June can handle things here for a while. If Sharon needs me, I couldn't say no. She was so good to me while I was sick last year."

The static on the phone crackled, and June leaned close, but couldn't make out her uncle's words.

"I'll take the bus," Anne continued. "As soon as I know the arrival time, I'll call you back." She hung up quietly.

Franklin shuffled into the living room. "You're going somewhere?" he asked with a scowl.

"My sister, Sharon, just had emergency gall bladder surgery. Bill says she's really sick." Anne wrapped her arms around herself and shivered. "I told him I'd nurse her when she comes home from the hospital. It sounds as if they really need me to come."

Trying to ignore her lurching stomach, June studied the African violets in the window. "How long will you be gone?"

"Unless there are complications, probably just a week. Maybe a little less." Her mom glanced up at Franklin, then blinked hastily, as if suddenly remembering something. "Oh, Franklin, I should have asked you first. I just didn't think. Will you two be all right if I go?"

June stroked the violet's velvety leaf. It would be lonely, but she guessed she could handle the house for a week. When her mom had been sick, she'd done all the cooking and cleaning anyway. She glanced at Franklin. As long as he didn't try to take his heart medicine too often, they'd survive.

Probably.

Franklin cleared his throat. "You go. You should be with your sister." Awkwardly he patted Anne's arm. "Don't worry. I'll take care of June."

June gasped. She didn't know whether to laugh or be mad. Franklin take care of *her*? *He* was the one who needed to be watched like a hawk.

Her mom squeezed Franklin's arm. "Thank you. I know I'm leaving June in good hands."

"Good hands?" June started to protest, but the words trailed off when her mom winked. Obviously she was supposed to go along with Franklin. Hope I can pull it off, June thought. It would be tricky to take care of Franklin, while pretending he was taking care of *her*.

On Thursday night after Franklin went to bed, June's mom sat beside her on the couch. "I've hidden Franklin's heart medicine in the kitchen cupboard. I'll show you where it is later." She sipped a cup of herbal tea. "You know how he sometimes forgets that he took it?"

June nodded. Franklin's medicine was to be taken only once in the morning, but sometimes he tried to take it more often during the day. "He's broken several dishes, I know, when looking for the medicine bottle."

"That's right. Even with the medicine hidden, there's a chance he could find it while you're at school or asleep at night." She held out a list. "I've written down the symptoms Doctor Thompson said to look for if you suspect he's taken too much medicine. The right amount of medicine slows his racing heartbeat and strengthens it. An overdose of the medicine would slow down his heart rate too much."

June scanned the list. *Nausea and vomiting. A very bad headache. Slow movements. Sleepiness.* "Don't worry, Mom. I'll watch Franklin real close."

On Friday after school, June blinked back tears as she watched her mom board the bus at the depot. When Anne's face appeared at the window, June smiled and waved gaily. If only she felt as brave as she tried to look.

She glanced at Franklin, standing statuelike beside her. After waving till the bus disappeared around the corner, they turned and trudged the six blocks home in the deepening twilight. June pulled her coat collar higher against the wind, noting how October's blazing orange and red leaves had given way to November's bare trees and low-hanging gray clouds.

Franklin's steps slowed the last two blocks. In spite of the biting wind, June resisted the urge to tell him to hurry. When they reached the corner of Brewster and Fourth, his dragging feet scuffed loudly on the sidewalk. June worried that the walk had been too much for him.

Just then a screen door banged. "*Yoo-hoo!* Oh, Franklin, dear!" Maybelle sang out.

Franklin's head jerked up, and he whirled around frantically.

"Guess what kind of pie I made today?" Maybelle called from her front steps. A ruffly apron was tied around her ample middle. "I baked it just for you!"

"Argh!" Franklin snarled. With new spring in his step, he turned and strode briskly up his sidewalk to the porch. Wheezing, he escaped into the house, the door slamming behind him.

Embarrassed, June walked to the edge of the street. "Hi, Maybelle," she called across.

Maybelle's disappointed face resembled a fallen soufflé. "Where's your mother? I saw you leave earlier. Why didn't she come back with you?"

"She went to Cincinnati for a few days. Her sister there had surgery and needs some nursing."

"I'm sorry to hear that." Suddenly Maybelle's face lit up. "You're not to worry. Not one itsy bitsy smidgen. You'll need some help with Anne gone, and I'd be delighted . . ."

"Thanks, but Mom left tons of food for us. We won't have to cook all week." That was true. The refrigerator held neatly labeled containers of prepared food. Oatmeal cookies and a raisin cake sat in the freezer, just needing to be thawed out.

"Oh, but you'll be busy with schoolwork. You don't want to worry about meals." She clapped her plump hands together, like an overgrown baby playing pat-a-cake. "I could bake a different kind of pie every day. Let's see, I'll start with rhubarb tomorrow, then have blueberry the next. . . ."

"No, really. Mom left us lots of food." June waved, eager to escape. "See you later, Maybelle."

In the house, June unbuttoned her coat as she wandered through the living room, dining room, and kitchen. All were empty.

"Franklin?"

She peeked out the back door, but the dark yard appeared empty. It was only six-thirty. Surely he hadn't gone to bed already. While hanging up her coat, there was a sudden crash in the bathroom. June raced down the hall. The door was ajar, and she pushed it open.

"Are you all right?" Her heart hammered. "What happened?"

Franklin pointed to some orange liquid splashed in the sink where a bottle had broken. "It slipped."

June dropped the broken decongestant bottle into the garbage. With a wet Kleenex, she wiped out the broken slivers of glass, then rinsed the sink.

"Is your nose stuffy?" she asked.

"No!"

"Then why did you want the decongestant?"

Franklin stared at the tile floor, refusing to answer. Casting about for the right words, June tried again.

"Were you looking for something?"

"None of your business," Franklin snapped. "This is still my house."

June blinked, trying not to take his comment personally. "I know. I just wanted to help."

"Then get my heart medicine. Where is it?"

Avoiding Franklin's accusing stare, June rinsed the clean sink again. "You already had your medicine, remember?" Her heart hammered. She really didn't want a scene with Franklin already. "You took it this morning before I went to school."

"I need more now."

June put two fingers on Franklin's skinny wrist to feel his pulse. It *was* racing a bit. "Do you feel sick?"

He snatched his arm away. "My heart's beating too fast, that's all."

"Your heart could be pounding from the way you raced into the house earlier," June agreed. She closed the medicine cabinet. Maybe she could joke him out of his cranky mood. "Say! Perhaps it's the sight of the lovely Maybelle that sets your pulse to racing. She *is* a charming lady."

At that suggestion, Franklin turned purple. June quickly filled a glass of water, fearing she had gone too far. "Just joking, Franklin, just joking."

He stomped out of the bathroom to his room across the hall and slammed the door. June sighed. Why did her efforts with him always seem to backfire?

June leaned against his bedroom door and knocked softly. "Come on, Franklin, I'm sorry. Let's go eat supper." No response. "Mom left some sliced chicken for sandwiches. You're probably just hungry." She waited, but still got no answer.

Sighing, she went and made two sandwiches, in case he changed his mind. Balanced on the step stool, she checked behind the extra sugar and flour for his heart medicine. It was still there. Her mom even changed hiding places every few days. Now June understood why.

Over the weekend, she did her best to fill her mom's shoes, but Franklin was critical of everything June did. She tried to keep in mind that he was just "keeping an eye on her," but by Sunday night he'd nearly driven her batty.

At noon that day, he wouldn't eat the potato salad she'd made. He was sure it had sat on the table too long before lunch. He muttered something about the mayonnaise "going bad." He wouldn't let June eat any either, which exasperated her, especially after the hour she'd spent making it. Before she could sneak a bite, he'd dumped it in the garbage.

Both Friday and Saturday nights he'd crawled out of bed twice, although June had assured him she'd locked the back door. Praying that he wouldn't fall and break a hip, June had listened from her bed each night as he crashed his way around the furniture to the kitchen and back.

On Saturday, when Whistler had called about a math assignment, Franklin had ordered June off the phone. "Your mother might be trying to get through to see how we are," he'd said. But the phone hadn't rung again, and Franklin had moped around the house the rest of the day, wondering aloud why Anne didn't call.

By Monday morning June couldn't wait to go to school. After giving Franklin his heart medicine, she hid it on the highest shelf in her bedroom closet, behind a hatbox full of yarn scraps. Glancing at the clock, she raced to the kitchen to check Franklin's food one last time.

June poked her head inside the refrigerator. Her voice sounded hollow. "I have to go in a second, Franklin. Let me show you what's here for lunch."

Franklin peered over her shoulder. "What's that?" he asked suspiciously.

"A scoop of chicken salad. Mom made it before she left." June pointed clockwise around the plate. "Plus half a peach, some raw carrots, and cottage cheese." She shut the refrigerator. "There's still cake in the pan on the counter."

Franklin cleared his throat. "Your mother went to a lot of trouble."

Surprised at his gentle tone, June slipped her small hand into his gnarled one. "You miss Mom, too, don't you?"

Franklin squeezed her fingers, then turned away. "Anne is good company."

June was lonely too, but if she talked about it, she was afraid she'd cry. "She'll be home before we . . ."

Thunderous pounding on the front door interrupted them. June hurried to let Sandy in.

"Are you coming?" Sandy asked, wrapped clear to her eyeballs in an orange scarf. "You're late."

"Sorry. I had some extra things to do. Let me get my coat." Head down, she rummaged in the hall closet for her mittens.

Franklin shuffled into the living room. He eyed Sandy with a suspicious glare, then pointed to the clock on the piano. It said 7:30. "Where are your manners? It's too early for social calls."

Sandy peered through the ruffled curtains toward the bus stop, then flopped down on the couch. "If I came any later, we'd *both* miss the bus. Anyway, this isn't a social call."

Franklin drew himself up, his nostrils flaring. "In

my day, young whippersnappers didn't talk back. They respected their elders."

Nervously jamming on her mittens, June whirled around to hustle Sandy out the door and soothe her hurt feelings. But she needn't have worried.

"Young whippersnapper? No manners?" Tassels flying, Sandy shook her scarf at Franklin. "You know something? You haven't changed a bit since your crabby days at Reed's Retirement Ranch!"

Franklin grabbed the back of the rocker for support. "Crabby, was I? Who wouldn't be, with kids invading the ranch, trampling the flowers, screaming and . . ."

"Of all the nerve! We came out there to cheer you old guys up!" Sandy stepped close to Franklin, her nose just inches from his. "As if we didn't have better things to do than sit and twiddle our thumbs and listen to boring stories about the olden days."

Frozen in her tracks, June looked on in horror, helpless to stop the fight. She knew she'd be sick to her stomach in a minute.

Franklin's wheezing words came out in a splutter. "There was nothing wrong with the olden days. Young upstarts were respectful then and held their tongues."

Sandy flung her scarf around her neck twice. "Oh, who cares?" she muttered from under her scarf. Without a backward glance, she flounced out the door.

"Sandy! Wait!" June grabbed her duffel bag and ran after her, then stopped and turned at the door. "Don't be mad at her, Franklin. Please. She just didn't want me to miss the bus." She opened the door a crack. "It's at the corner now! I have to go."

June jumped off the porch and raced to the bus stop, hoping her churning stomach would calm down soon. Sandy was her best friend, but she loved Franklin. She hated being caught in the middle of their arguments. It was like being squeezed in a vise.

Slumping into the seat beside Sandy, June shrugged and shook her head. At least Sandy didn't hold a grudge. It was one thing for June to accept Franklin's behavior. But how long could she ask her friends to do the same?

At lunchtime she'd almost forgotten about Franklin. Head down, she tried to concentrate on her cafeteria spaghetti. The meat in the sauce was, as usual, impossible to identify.

"Hi, June."

At the sound of Whistler's voice, June glanced up happily. Her smile stretched to a grin as she studied Whistler's new emerald green jogging suit, complete with racing stripes up the legs. Instead of the school's spaghetti and garlic bread, he carried a brown paper bag. "Mind if I sit down?"

"Go ahead." June tried to ignore the sudden fluttering in her stomach. "I only have a couple minutes though. I promised to help shelve some new books in the library."

June watched as Whistler sucked in his stomach, threw back his shoulders, marched to the seat across from her, and sat down. From his lunch sack he pulled a carton of vanilla low-fat yogurt and a plastic spoon.

He looked at June's leftover garlic bread, sighed, then peeled the lid from the yogurt container.

"What's with the yogurt and jogging suit?" June asked after he'd forced down three bites.

Sheepishly, Whistler stirred his spoon around and around in his yogurt. "Maybe you haven't noticed, but I'm bigger than a lot of the kids in our class." He looked up hopefully.

"I hadn't noticed." June glanced at his double chin, then looked away quickly. "Well, I hardly noticed."

"Well, not for long," Whistler declared. "I'm jogging to school every morning and back home in the afternoon. That's a whole mile altogether." He nodded vigorously, his extra chin wobbling. "And look at this." He unzipped his jacket. Stuck to his T-shirt was a pin that read "I'm Allergic to Food: It Makes Me Break Out In Fat."

June smiled. "I admire what you're doing, Whistler. I bet that takes a lot of discipline." She glanced up at the clock. "Gotta go. See you in geometry."

An hour later, June had just arranged her test tubes of salt solution when the school secretary bustled into the science room.

After a whispered conference, Mr. Myers, the science teacher, hurried over to June's work station. "You have a phone call in the office. The secretary says to bring your books with you."

June froze. When the secretary finally picked up her books for her, June followed her out of the room. Her footsteps were muffled by the secretary's clicking heels.

"Who's on the phone? My mom?"

"It's a lady, but I got the impression she was a friend."

Puzzled, June picked up the phone in the principal's office. "Yes? Hello?"

"Juney? It's Maybelle."

"Maybelle? What . . ."

"You'd better come home quick. Something's happened to Franklin."

"Oh, no! Is he okay?"

"I don't know. You'd better hurry home." The connection was broken with a sharp *click*.

Alarmed, June explained the problem to the principal and got permission to leave the building. She didn't even stop by her locker for her coat, and barely noticed the icy November wind in her face.

What could have happened to Franklin? Had he fallen when climbing on a chair? Maybe even broken a hip? Or had he found his heart medicine and taken some more? *What could have happened to Franklin?* The question went round and round in her head like a broken record.

By the time she reached home, she was bending over from a stitch in her side. June half expected to see a fire engine or an ambulance parked at the curb. Instead, Maybelle was on their front porch, peering through the living room windows.

June panted as she climbed the steps. "I got here as soon as I could. What's the matter with Franklin?"

"I don't know." Maybelle craned her plump neck to peer around the edge of the curtains. "I don't see him. I've tried to get a response all afternoon. First I rang the bell over and over, but he didn't open the door. So I went home and called on the phone four or five times, but there was no answer." She wrung her plump hands together. "Do you suppose it's his heart?"

June rattled the doorknob.

Maybelle hovered over her shoulder. "It's locked. I already tried. So is the back door."

With trembling fingers, June fished her house key out of her billfold. In ten seconds she was inside. Just as Maybelle had claimed, the living room was empty. June raced down the hallway, but the bedrooms and bathroom were empty too. Rounding the corner into the dining room, she halted abruptly. The heavy drapes were pulled, and Franklin was sitting in the corner of the dim room, bony hands clasped between his knees.

Weak-kneed, June knelt down beside him. "Franklin?" she whispered. "Are you hurt? Are you in pain?"

He mumbled something, but June couldn't make out his words.

"What did you say?"

He edged closer to her ear. "I'm hiding."

June sat back on her heels. Had Franklin finally flipped his lid? What kind of danger could he be hiding from?

"*Yoo-hoo!* Franklin? Juney?"

Franklin jerked back in his chair and waved his hands frantically. His eyes opened wide, and they rolled from side to side. At Franklin's panicky reaction, the light suddenly dawned. June knew who he was cowering from in the dark: *Maybelle.*

She hurried to the living room where Maybelle stood

in the open door. "I found him. Franklin just needs some rest. Thanks for calling me."

Exhausted from being scared to death, June went back to sit by Franklin. She had no idea what to say to him. How could he be so terror-stricken by Maybelle? She *did* come on strong, June had to admit to herself, but she seemed harmless enough.

June patted Franklin's knee. "It's okay. She's gone. As long as I'm home early, we might as well have a snack and play some checkers."

As she headed toward the kitchen for a box of graham crackers, soft piano music floated in from the living room. "Oh, no!" June thought, whirling around. Maybelle had sneaked inside instead of leaving.

Maybelle's dramatic voice rose and fell sorrowfully. "I love you truly, truly dear. Life with its sorrows, life with its tears. . . ."

June glanced over her shoulder. Poor Franklin! The whites of his eyes showed clearly in the darkened room. His bony knuckles gripped the sides of his chair, and his mouth opened and closed wordlessly.

Then, as Maybelle's warbling voice climbed to new heights, June just couldn't help it. She scurried from the room to hide the laughter that bubbled out.

7

The Banquet

❦❦❦

*T*he bell rang at the end of Thursday's home-ec class, just as June glued the last glittered feather on her Styrofoam turkey. Head cocked to one side, she stood back to study it, then went to wash up. Maybe a turkey wasn't too original for a Thanksgiving centerpiece, but hers was as pretty as those her friends had made.

In spite of her mom's absence, the week had passed quickly for June. The Father-Daughter Banquet was on Friday night, and she'd used her study hall hours all week to make table and window decorations. That meant extra homework to drag home at night, keeping June too busy to miss her mom. At least, not *too* much.

With a last glance at her turkey, June headed out the door. Ms. Buckingham caught her arm. "Could I see you a minute, June?"

"Sure." June followed her teacher back to her desk.

"I have a slight problem about tomorrow night. You've worked so hard on the table centerpieces that I almost hate to ask."

"Ask what?"

"Well, Stacy Enright has the mumps, of all things. I didn't think kids got that anymore." Disgustedly, she tapped a long silver-painted fingernail against her polished desk top. "She was supposed to help cook for the banquet."

"You want me to take her place?"

"If you could, I'd be indebted to you." She riffled through a stack of papers to the sign-up sheet. "Let's see. Stacy was supposed to cook glazed carrots. They're not hard. I'll have a simple recipe for you."

Students began to file in for the next home-ec class. June glanced at the clock. She barely had a minute to get to science class. "I've never made glazed carrots before, but I guess I could try."

Ms. Buckingham flashed a dazzling smile. "I knew I could count on you. Be in the cafeteria by 4:30. That should give you plenty of time to fix the glazed carrots before the banquet starts at 6:30."

She shook her finger at two boys who were arm wrestling on top of a stove. Embarrassed by the eighth graders' stares, June edged toward the door, ready to make a dash for it.

Ms. Buckingham's shrill voice rose over the chattering students. "I'll be in the kitchen tomorrow night if you have questions. The carrots and ingredients for the glaze will be there. Just come prepared to work."

"Okay," June called over her shoulder as she dashed down the hall. Luckily the science room was on the same floor. She slid into her work station as the final bell rang.

The next day after school, June changed from her fuzzy sweater into an old, faded pink sweatshirt, suitable for glazing carrots in the school kitchen.

"I'll be back about 6:30," she said to Franklin, bundling up in her coat and scarf against the thirty-degree temperature.

Franklin peered over the top of his newspaper. "Where are you going?" he asked, his voice less brusque than usual.

Sitting in the pool of lamplight, June thought his craggy features appeared softened. He *was* more patient with her since she'd rescued him from Maybelle and convinced her to leave him alone during the day. As tempting as it was to tease him, June had never once referred to his hiding from Maybelle in the dining room.

"I have a home-ec project to work on," June answered, careful to tell him the truth without actually mentioning the banquet. "I'll be at school if you need me. I left the number by the phone. There's meat loaf to reheat for supper when I get back."

By the time she reached school, her fingertips and nose were numb. The kitchen's warmth nearly overpowered her after fighting the gusting November wind.

"Oh, there you are, June!" In one swift motion, Ms. Buckingham snatched her coat and steered her to a stainless steel sink. "Start by peeling the two bags of carrots in that refrigerator. Here's the knife and the peeler. Slice the carrots into quarter-inch slices. When these two pans are full, tell me, and I'll explain how to make the glaze." Without waiting for a reply, she swooped down on the next volunteer coming through the door.

June glanced around the noisy kitchen. In one corner, Suzy Atkins was scooping out orange halves and filling each rind with cranberry sauce. At the center work table, a student teacher mixed spices and torn-up bread.

"Hi, June!"

Holly waved as she whizzed by, her long frizzy hair trailing in clouds behind her. At the relish table, Ms. Buckingham showed her how to make radish roses and cucumber pinwheels. Holly nodded so vigorously through the demonstration that the teacher jammed a net down on her head to control her hair.

For a moment, June closed her eyes and breathed deeply. The aroma of the three turkeys roasting in the oven made her stomach growl. If she pretended hard enough, she could imagine she was part of a big, happy family, all cooking Thanksgiving dinner together.

When she reluctantly opened her eyes, she caught Ms. Buckingham's frown. Hastily she opened the refrigerator to get the two bags of carrots. At first she couldn't spot them. Then she saw two paper sacks shoved behind the pitchers of tropical punch.

She peered into one. Somehow she'd pictured two

small plastic bags of carrots, the size she bought at the store for her mom. Pulling the sacks out of the refrigerator, she guessed each bag weighed a good five pounds. June sighed. She'd be slicing and peeling forever.

Dumping the first bagful in the sink, June grabbed the peeler and got to work. Slivers of carrot skin flew right and left. Actually, it wasn't bad. Someone had brought a radio, but June just listened to those talking around her. It was nice to be in a group, even on the fringes. She was glad after all that she'd agreed to help out with the banquet, even if she couldn't go as a guest.

An hour later June had the carrots sliced and on the stove to boil. As she stirred the carrots, she wiggled her left foot to warm it up. Earlier, Sandy Hanes had tripped while carrying a pitcher of tropical fruit punch. Red liquid had splattered all over the floor, including June's jeans and left foot. Now she had one white tennis shoe and one pink-streaked one.

When the carrots were fork tender, Ms. Buckingham showed June how to make the glaze. The bubbling butter and brown sugar mixture soon added to the other heavenly smells. June was beginning to envy the girls going to the banquet. Her cold meat loaf at home sounded bland by comparison.

June glanced at her watch. Six-fifteen already! She'd better get home.

Ms. Buckingham was slicing turkey on the cutting board while the others cleaned up. June put her sugary carrots on simmer and turned to get her coat from the hook.

In the kitchen doorway stood Franklin, holding a crumpled paper sack.

June hurried over to him. "Is everything all right?" she asked. "Did Mom call or something?" She couldn't imagine why he'd gone out in the freezing weather to come to school.

Silently, Franklin backed out into the cafeteria, now strung with orange and yellow crepe-paper streamers. Pumpkins and gourds were piled in the corners, while the table decorations made in home ec added a holiday feeling.

"What's wrong?" June asked again.

"Nothing." Franklin handed her the crumpled sack. "Here."

Puzzled, June opened the paper sack. Wadded up inside was her favorite Sunday dress. It was red, with white ribbons laced through the hem and sleeves. She looked up at Franklin. Although he didn't smile, she could swear his eyes twinkled a little.

"I don't understand, Franklin."

"Here. I bought these at the door." He held out two tickets, the words "Father-Daughter Banquet" printed in fancy letters.

June's stomach suddenly did a nose dive to the bottom of her shoes. *Now* she understood. In return for her protection against Maybelle, Franklin had bought tickets to the banquet. He'd even brought her a dress to wear.

"How did you know?" she finally asked, her voice small and thin.

"Your friend—the big one—he called to talk to you."

"Whistler?"

Franklin nodded. "When I said you were working at school, he remembered the banquet. Said it was for fathers and daughters."

June stared at her mismatched shoes, too ashamed to meet Franklin's eyes. What must he think of her, now that he knew about the banquet and that she hadn't invited him?

She picked a dried carrot peeling off her shirt. "I just came to cook. I wasn't going to stay and eat."

"Now you can." Franklin cleared his gravelly throat several times. "I know I'm not your father, but the lady selling tickets said grandfathers were all right too."

Breathing heavily, Franklin fell silent, as if his unusually long speech had exhausted him.

June bit her lower lip as she watched the cafeteria begin to fill. Handsome fathers in suits and ties were escorting pretty daughters, most of whom wore dresses and hose, even heels. She could tell by the feel of the sack that Franklin had forgotten her dressy shoes.

Franklin seemed so pleased with what he had done. Staring at the tickets in her hand, June knew she could hardly refuse.

June held up the sack and lifted her chin. "I'll run to the restroom and change. I'll be back in a minute." She turned to go, then hesitated. "Um, thank you, Franklin," she said, trying to sound enthusiastic, but failing miserably.

Ten minutes later, she forced herself to leave the

sanctuary of the girls' restroom and return to the cafeteria. Her wet tennis shoe squeaked with each step. Franklin had also forgotten her slip, and the dress was full of static. With each step, she peeled away the skirt from where it clung to her bare legs.

Staring straight ahead, she fought waves of embarrassment. From the snickers she heard, June figured the other girls thought she was color-blind. Her red and white dress, although wrinkled, was becoming. But combined with mismatched, pink-stained tennis shoes, and no socks, she felt bedraggled.

When she reached the cafeteria doorway, she hung back around the corner, hunting for Franklin. Finally she spotted him, partly hidden by a sheaf of yellow cornstalks. Clutching his hat, he looked lost and alone. His black coat and nearly bald head made him appear even thinner and more bent than he was.

With a jolt, June realized he didn't really want to be there at all. He had only come to the banquet for her.

June straightened her shoulders and ran fingers through her uncombed hair. Then, taking a deep breath, she squeaked across the floor in her damp, multicolored tennis shoes. She slipped her hand into the crook of Franklin's arm, smiled, and led him to their table.

Lying in bed that night, June admitted to herself that the banquet had been every bit as awkward as she'd feared. Tongue-tied and uncomfortable, Franklin had replied with grunts and snorts whenever a father asked him a question. Finally the other men gave up and just talked over his bent head.

Although the food had been delicious and should have made her mouth water, June could barely swallow it. Even her sugary glazed carrots lay in a rock-hard lump in her stomach.

Rolling over, she plumped up her pillow. If her mother were there, June knew what she'd say. She could almost hear her advice: "Appreciate Franklin's thoughtfulness, June, and don't worry about how it turned out. Franklin's good intentions are what matter."

June burrowed further under her quilt and sighed guiltily. "Maybe Franklin *is* trying to change," she admitted to herself. "I guess he's just too old to be who I really need."

June went to the station alone on Sunday afternoon to meet her mom's bus. When Anne came slowly down the steps, June was alarmed at the black circles around her eyes and the deep lines beside her mouth.

She hurried forward to take the small carryall. "Mom, are you all right?" She hugged her carefully, suddenly afraid her fragile mother might break.

"I'm fine. It was a long trip." Anne pulled her coat tighter. "It's so good to be home." She briefly laid a cool hand on June's cheek.

They headed for home after June collected her mom's suitcase. "How's Aunt Sharon?" she asked.

"Oh, much better. And much thinner. You'd hardly recognize her."

June nodded, recalling the last time she'd seen her plump aunt. "Did she require a lot of nursing?"

"Yes, especially at first. But by the time I left, Bill could manage everything that she needed."

Her voice trailed off rather forlornly. June wondered if she were remembering her own illness the previous summer, wishing *her* husband had been able to be with her.

They walked the next block in silence. June stopped and flexed her stiff fingers, then switched the suitcase to her other hand.

When they were just a block from Franklin's house, her mom stopped right in the middle of the sidewalk. "You know, June, I don't think I could ever live with Bill and Sharon."

June glanced up in surprise. "Didn't Uncle Bill make you feel welcome?"

"Oh, yes, very much." She smiled wanly. "But, you see, once Sharon felt a little better, they didn't need me any more. They have each other." Sighing, she rubbed her chapped hands together. "They will always have each other. I want to be where I'm *needed* by people."

They paused in front of Franklin's house. A lamp already glowed in the living room window.

Anne sighed. Her words came out in barely more than a whisper. "Franklin needs me here, June. He really does. It just *has* to work out."

June bit her bottom lip. She'd planned to tell her mom all about the embarrassing Father-Daughter Banquet the minute she was unpacked. But how could she now? From the sounds of things, living with Franklin was the only choice that would make her mom happy.

However, June thought, following her mom up the sidewalk, where did that leave *her*?

8
Hard As Clay

❦ ❦ ❦

June stamped her feet to warm up her numb toes, glad they were almost home. Even though the first snow of the year was melting, it was still cold for a walk. Now that her mom was back home, she was giving piano lessons again.

Glancing sideways at Franklin, June was almost sorry she'd volunteered to keep him busy during her mom's lessons. When she'd come up with the idea back in September, she hadn't considered the winter weather.

Abruptly Franklin swerved and left the sidewalk.

"Where are you going?" June called.

Without answering, Franklin continued to trudge across the adjoining backyards. June shrugged. For some reason he wanted to go in the back door. Heaven knows why, June thought. It was a lot easier walking to the front door on the sidewalk than cutting across the rolling backyards.

Suddenly June grinned. She bet she knew. Franklin was avoiding the front of the house—and Maybelle's watchful eyes. June knew he was counting the days until Maybelle finally returned home to Minnesota.

Strains of "Camptown Races" met June as she followed Franklin through the back door. She glanced at the kitchen clock. Five minutes were left of the student's lesson.

"Want to play checkers?" June whispered.

Franklin nodded, removing his rubbers, but keeping his black hat and coat on. As June set up the game, Franklin lingered in the living-room doorway. His bony hands clapped silently in rhythm with the piano.

June peered around the corner. The student's mother was sitting on the couch, purse on her lap. Smiling slightly, her eyes were closed as she nodded in time with the music.

Except it was hard to keep steady time. The little girl had to start over repeatedly. She played perfectly during "Camptown ladies sing this song," but the "Doodahs" gave her trouble. June marveled at her mom's patience as the little girl repeated the first line over and over.

Ready to play checkers, June tugged on Franklin's sleeve. He ignored her and continued to clap softly while mouthing the words. "Camptown ladies sing this song . . ." But the little girl just couldn't do the "Doodahs."

"Slow down, dear." June's mother pointed to the notes. "You're rushing it here. The *doo* has one count, but the *dah* has three counts."

When she tried but played it wrong again, Franklin shook his head vigorously. "No, no, no!" He shuffled over to the piano. "Like this: 'Doo-*daaahhh*, Doo-*daaahhh*,'" he croaked.

The little girl stared wide-eyed at him.

Anne smiled uncomfortably at the girl's mother, who had edged forward on the couch. "Thank you, Franklin. I'm sure Josie has the rhythm now."

Josie tried again, while June's mom sang along. "Camptown ladies sing this song, Doo-daaahhh, Doo-daaahhh. Camptown racetrack's five miles long. Oh, doo-dah day." Josie still missed the timing, finishing two measures ahead of June's mom.

Franklin shook his head and stomped over to the couch. "You her mother?" he demanded.

The woman blinked. "Yes, I am."

"Someone should tell you. You're wasting your money." Franklin pointed a gnarled finger at the girl. "No rhythm."

Inwardly June groaned. The banquet had led June to think Franklin was changing, but evidently, once a black key, always a black key. "Franklin! Come on. I've got the game all set up." She led him away, but not before she saw Josie's stricken expression or the mother's grim one.

Feeling guilty, June was mad at herself for letting Franklin interrupt the lesson. He hadn't done anything like that since scaring away the Lyons boy several weeks ago. Still, she should have been on her toes. Franklin had lulled her into a false sense of security, but she had only herself to blame.

Thanksgiving came and went the next week, with little fanfare. They'd been invited out to Reed's Retirement Ranch for Thanksgiving dinner, but they'd all agreed that they wanted to spend their first Thanksgiving alone together. They had roast chicken instead of turkey, but no one seemed to mind.

The following Saturday it snowed. Not just a measly inch or two that left brown grass sticking through, but eight whole inches. Scalloped drifts piled high against the house. The porch rails and swing were quilted with three inches of white padding.

"I'm dreaming of a white Christmas," June sang as she stared out the window.

That afternoon, while both her mom and Franklin napped, June decided to get the box of Christmas ornaments down from the closet. She didn't know if Franklin owned any or not, but they'd brought all theirs with them. With the snow falling gently outside, it seemed the perfect time to decorate.

Soon she'd dusted each carved figure for the wooden Nativity scene and arranged them on top of the piano. Then, while digging in the cardboard box, she found a fat Christmas candle and some plastic poinsettias.

I know what I could make with these, June thought.

In her bedroom, she dug out the modeling clay left

over from her art project. Then, at the kitchen table, she rolled the clay into a snake and wrapped it around the base of the green candle. While the clay was still soft, she stuck in the plastic flowers. Soon she had a ring of poinsettias circling the base of the candle.

"Oohh, that's pretty."

June swung around at the sound of her mom's voice. "I didn't know you were up. Have a nice nap?"

"Slept like a baby." Her mom stretched her arms high over her head. "Franklin not up yet?"

June shook her head and carried the candle to the windowsill to dry. If the sun came out later, the clay would harden in no time.

"Sure you want that candle in a south window?" her mom asked. "It reminds me of an old proverb my grandmother used to say whenever she had a problem: 'The sun that melts the wax, hardens the clay.' "

June rolled bits of leftover clay into little balls. "I don't get it."

"Oh, just that the hot sun will both melt your candle *and* harden the clay at the same time. In a broader sense it means that difficulties come to us all, just like the sun shines down on everyone. Some people grow hard and brittle, like the clay. Others become soft and bendable—like the wax—letting their problems change them for the better."

June moved the candle out of the window. "You're really talking about Franklin, aren't you?"

Her mom nodded slowly. "I was really angry after his comment to my student's mother last week. And I know he says things that embarrass you in front of your friends."

June picked up the flower scraps. "So what do we do?"

"I guess we'd better be flexible and bendable, like the wax."

"There's not much choice," June agreed, "because Franklin sure is one *hard* piece of clay."

Laughing, June and her mom went into the living room to set out the rest of the Christmas decorations.

That night after supper, June waited anxiously until Franklin had gone to bed. Hovering outside his door, she finally heard his first snores.

With a sigh of relief, she sneaked into the kitchen and dragged a chair over to the telephone. Flipping open the phone book, she skimmed through the short list of Norths. Knowing Whistler's address, it was easy to figure out which was his number.

With shaky fingers, she dialed the first three digits before abruptly hanging up.

Her mom peeked around the edge of the doorway. "Did you call yet?"

"I'm going to in a minute." June took several deep breaths to calm her pounding heart.

Anne Finch grinned. "You'll do fine." With a thumbs-up signal, she left the room.

June dialed again, letting the phone ring this time. After weeks of thinking about it, she'd finally decided to invite Whistler to the girl-ask-boy Christmas dance at school. At the time it had sounded easy, since they were just good friends. He wasn't her *boyfriend* or anything, June told herself sternly. There was no reason for her palms to be so clammy that she could barely hang on to the phone.

"North residence," a lady's voice said.

June cleared her throat. "Um, is Whistler there? I mean, um, Myron North?"

There was a short pause before the lady said, "I'll get him."

June stretched the telephone cord behind her as she paced back and forth across the tiny kitchen. What if Whistler was already going to the dance with someone else? She'd just die. June shook her head. Surely she was asking early enough. The dance was still three weeks away. Still, what if he didn't want to take her because Franklin was so mean to him? What if . . .

"Hi. Whistler here."

"Um, hi." She tried to swallow the lump in her throat. "How'd you like the new snow?" June finally asked, putting off the moment when he'd turn down her invitation.

Whistler's words were punctuated by little gasps. "It's okay . . . *gasp* . . . if you're . . ." *gasp* . . . an Eskimo."

"An Eskimo! Oh, that's funny!" Even to her own ears, June's laugh sounded slightly false.

"Whatcha need?"

June took a deep breath. "Well, actually, I want to ask you something."

At the sound of shuffling steps in the hallway, June froze. With pajama legs flapping, Franklin padded into the kitchen and ran the tap for a glass of water.

"You wanted to ask me something?" Whistler prompted her, breathing heavily.

"Uh, yes." June wondered at Whistler's breathlessness. Was he that excited about her call? It was rather flattering.

"Well, what I mean is . . ." June watched Franklin slowly drain his glass. Then he rinsed it. Then he looked out the window and straightened the curtain. Wasn't he *ever* going to leave?

Turning, he blinked, as if just realizing June was in the room. He shuffled over to stand in front of her. "Who's on the phone?" he croaked.

June hastily covered the mouthpiece. "It's Whistler," she hissed.

"I didn't hear the phone ring."

June gulped. "It didn't. I called him."

"What!" Franklin reached for the phone, but June whipped it around behind her back. "Give me that. I won't have you chasing that boy!"

"Hush!" June gasped in horror at what she'd said. "I mean, please be quiet. Whistler will hear you." If he was still on the line, she thought. He must think she lived in a nuthouse.

Just then her mom appeared in the kitchen. "Oh, dear. Here, Franklin, let me fix you some nice herbal tea. You come wait in the rocker." She rolled her eyes at June.

"I don't want to," he mumbled. Still protesting, he let himself be led from the kitchen.

June collapsed on the chair wearily. "Whistler? You still there?"

93

"Yup." His heavy breathing nearly drowned out his words. "What was all that?"

"Nothing." She decided to take the plunge and get the rejection over with. "You don't want to go with me to the Christmas dance at school, do you? If you don't, I'll understand. I just thought . . ."

"I'll go."

"You will?"

"Sure. We have fun together. On one condition."

"What's that?"

"Don't bring Franklin!" Whistler burst out laughing, then wheezed breathlessly.

June wound the cord around her finger. Whistler sure sounded pleased that she'd called. Or was he as nervous as she was? He could hardly catch his breath. "Well, I'll let you get back to doing whatever I interrupted."

"No problem. I'm still doing it."

"Doing what?"

"My low impact aerobics. It's the latest thing. It's safer for you than jogging—easier on the joints." *Pant, pant.*

Sheepishly, June asked, "That's why you're breathing funny?"

"Yup. I'm still doing my routine. You can do it on the phone, or in front of TV, or anywhere. It uses wrist weights and lots of arm movement."

Deflated, June was grateful Whistler couldn't read her thoughts. "I'll let you get back to it now. Thanks, Whistler."

Grinning, June slowly replaced the receiver. Overwhelmed with relief, she suddenly was hungry. At supper she'd been too nervous to eat much, but now the leftover fried chicken would hit the spot.

With a plateful of food, she peeked around the corner of the living room. Only her mom was there, wrapped in a quilt, reading.

"Where's Franklin?" June whispered.

"He decided he was tired, after all. He's in bed." Her mom patted a spot on the couch beside her. "Come sit."

Now that the phone call was over and Whistler had accepted her invitation, June could laugh as she told about Franklin's behavior. "I wouldn't give him the phone. I was afraid he'd ask Whistler's intentions again!" Pressing a hand over her mouth, she tried to stifle her giggles. It only made it worse.

Her mom pointed to the candle encircled with June's red poinsettias. "Remember the clay and the wax?" she asked, patting June's knee. "I'm proud to say you're very waxy! Being able to laugh at yourself is one of the best ways to keep from turning into hard clay."

June glanced around the cozy room, noting the black sweater folded neatly in the rocker. "I can't always laugh, though. Sometimes I get so mad inside that I want to scream at him. Other times, I just want to sit down and cry. Suppose I'm nuts?"

"No, not nuts." Her mom winked at her. "At your age, your emotions go up and down like a roller coaster. It's perfectly normal."

"Well, with Franklin around, it's either laugh or go crazy," June replied, finishing her piece of cold chicken.

Holding out the greasy wishbone to her mom, June closed her eyes, made a wish, then broke the chicken bone. Triumphantly, she held up the larger piece.

9
Deck the Halls

❦❧❦

"H ere's the angel!" June unwrapped the lacy creation
from its tissue paper. Crawling up on a chair,
she fastened it on the highest branch of the tree.
"How's that?"

"Lovely." Eyes shining, her mom smiled up at her.

June caught her breath, trying to freeze in her mind
a picture of her mom's expression. Compared to last winter when she was frequently bent over with pain, she
now ate and rested well. She was still awfully thin, June
admitted to herself, but that glow in her cheeks made
her look radiant.

The last two weeks had been wonderful. They had
baked candy-cane cookies and decorated the house and
shopped for Christmas presents and sung carols around
the piano. Still, the warm glow she felt was from more

than those holiday activities. It was doing those things with special people. Together, with Franklin, they seemed like a real family.

"Where're our stockings?" June asked, climbing down to rummage in the cardboard box marked "XMAS."

"In that silver box over there. I didn't want them to get crushed." Anne Finch pointed to a large, flat container.

Since there was no crackling fireplace, they decided to hang the stockings on the end of the piano. June first taped up her mom's white stocking with red trim, then her own matching one.

"Where's your stocking, Franklin? I'll hang it up with ours."

"Bah." Franklin sat hunched over in the rocker, untangling strings of Christmas lights and muttering under his breath. "That's for children."

June's mom laughed. "*My* stocking's up. If you don't hang yours, you won't get any presents on Christmas morning."

"Wait! I know." June skipped down the hall and was back a minute later, waving something over her head. "I'll hang this. Sorry, but it's the only color I could find."

She smoothed out the black wrinkled knit sock she'd taken from Franklin's dresser drawer, then hung it limply beside her own. June frowned. "Talk about depressing," she said. Snapping her fingers, she dug out a silver bow and taped it to the black toe. "It looks ridiculous," she admitted, "but at least it's cheerier."

The shorter black stocking hanging between the two long white ones reminded June of piano keys. Silently she watched Franklin's gnarled fingers work at the tangled tree lights. Was it her imagination, June wondered, or were she and Franklin harmonizing a bit more these days? It was hard to tell—maybe she was simply getting used to the way they clashed.

A sharp rap on the door made Franklin drop the snarled Christmas lights. June hurried to the door. Wrapped in a green and red scarf, Whistler stood huddled on their porch.

June smoothed her flyaway hair and opened the door. "Hi, Whistler. Come on in." Flustered, she backed into the tree when shutting the door. Prickly pine needles scratched her bare arms.

"Hello, Whistler." June's mom sat cross-legged on the floor, unwrapping ornaments. "What brings you out on such a cold night?"

"Um, I was just walking by. Thought I'd stop and say hello." He glanced over at Franklin. The tangled tree lights were wrapped around his feet. "Good evening, Sir."

"Humph. What's good about it?"

Smiling at June, Whistler silently piled his coat and scarf on the couch, revealing bright blue weights wrapped around his ankles.

June pointed to his feet. "Are those what you wear for your low impact aerobics?" she asked. "They look heavy."

"Five pounds each," Whistler said proudly. "But I'm not doing the low impact aerobics anymore. It got boring staying in the house to exercise all the time. I can wear these everywhere."

"I thought you said jogging was too hard on your joints."

"It is. I'm in a walking program now. The weights give me even more of a workout." Whistler pulled up his sweatshirt to show June a watchlike instrument hooked to his belt. "This is a pedometer. It automatically records the distance I walk."

"How?"

"I don't know exactly. The man at the sporting-goods store said it responds to my body motion with each step." He strode quickly back and forth across the living room, his pedometer swaying with his ample stomach.

"Plenty of body motion," Franklin muttered into his tangled tree lights.

June gasped at his comment, but Whistler just shrugged and pulled his shirt down. Whistler didn't seem to be scared by Franklin's grouchiness. She was glad. If a person looked long enough, there *was* a soft side to Franklin, as she and her mother knew. It was rare for someone outside the family to see it too.

June began wrapping the gold roping around the base of the tree, inhaling the woodsy pine scent as she went. Scooting behind the tree with the roping, June hummed "Deck the Halls with Boughs of Holly." Soon her mom picked up the carol, and Whistler joined in on the last "fa-la-la-la-la, la-la, la, la."

Franklin, on the other hand, grew more and more irritated with the knotted string of Christmas lights. Finally he threw them on the floor and stomped out of the room and down the hall. They soon heard the bathroom door slam.

Reaching for more roping, June caught a glimpse of Whistler through the tree branches. As she watched, he quietly untangled the knots from the string of lights. At the muffled sound of running water, Whistler quickly piled the lights beside the rocker and went to hang ornaments on the tree.

Franklin shuffled back into living room and plopped down in his chair. June lowered a small branch to get a better view. When Franklin picked up the lights, he had them untangled in no time. Suspiciously he glanced up from under his bushy eyebrows. June let the branch slip back into place.

Franklin cleared his throat several times. "The lights are ready," he announced, bringing them to Anne. They were looped over his arm.

"Give them to June," Anne said, polishing a crystal handblown bell ornament. "I never was any good with the lights. In fact, June's done most of the decorating in the past."

June nodded, remembering the short trees they'd always bought, the inexpensive size that sat on a table to look bigger. This was the first time she remembered having a tree that nearly touched the ceiling. Franklin had had it delivered that morning.

June's mom shivered and pulled her sweater close about her. "I know. I'll make us some hot apple cider to have when we finish." With a wink in June's direction, she left the room.

Whistler stood on a chair to attach the colored lights,

starting with the top branches. "Hey, June, did you hear Suzy's version of 'Deck the Halls'?"

"No. What's that?"

"In science today everybody was singing it like this." He cleared his throat:

> Deck the halls with balls of cotton,
> fa-la-la-la-la, la-la, la, la.
> 'Tis the season to be rotten,
> fa-la-la-la-la, la-la, la, la.
> Break a window, pop a tire,
> fa-la-la, la-la-la, la, la, la.
> Set the Christmas tree on fire,
> fa-la-la-la-la, la-la, la, la.

June burst out laughing. "Just don't set *this* Christmas tree on fire!"

"That stinks."

June whirled around. "What did you say?"

Eyebrows drawn together, Franklin stared at Whistler. "That song stinks. And you're too fat to stand on my chair. Get down before you break it."

Hastily, Whistler climbed down off the chair. "Sorry." His red hair looked pale next to his fiery face.

"It's okay, Whistler," June whispered, feeling her own face flush hotly. Of all the rotten things to say!

Behind the tree, June stood with fists clenched. What was the matter with Franklin anyway? Whistler was only being helpful. Franklin almost acted jealous of her friends, as if he resented sharing her with anyone outside their family.

Franklin shuffled back to his rocker, then stared at them down the end of his hawk nose. June stared right back. That scowl didn't scare her anymore. She knew exactly what he was doing. He thought if he stared long enough, Whistler would get embarrassed and go home.

Well, June thought with determination, *not this time.* She'd been understanding long enough. This was the *last straw.*

With as much gusto as her reedy voice could muster, June sang out "Oh, Christmas Tree, Oh, Christmas Tree, Thy leaves are so unchanging." Ignoring Franklin, she chirped one carol after another. When her mom returned with a tray of cider mugs, she joined in too. By the last chorus of "We Wish You a Merry Christmas," Whistler's face was back to its normal color.

"*Yoo-hoo!* Anybody home?" The front door opened an inch, letting in a gust of frigid air and a few snowflakes. "I guess you didn't hear me over your singing."

Maybelle, adorned with a white fur hat and muff, bounced into the living room, shaking the ornaments on the tree. With her bright red coat, she reminded June of Mrs. Santa Claus. Rather than going home after Thanksgiving as planned, Maybelle had decided to stay with her grandchildren until after Christmas.

Franklin threw himself forward out of his chair and edged toward the hall, but the doorway was blocked by decoration boxes piled high. The dining-room doorway was blocked by the Christmas tree, pulled out into the room to decorate. Turning this way and that, Franklin reminded June of a cornered rabbit.

Instinctively, June started to go to his rescue. She could probably get rid of Maybelle again, just like the day June had been called home early from school.

Then, remembering all the embarrassing comments Franklin had hurled at Whistler, Sandy, and her mom's piano students, she squelched the impulse. Franklin hadn't toned down his blunt remarks at all. Accepting his behavior hadn't made him change one bit, no matter what her mom believed. Maybe, just once, he should have to fend for himself. Franklin *might* change if he got a taste of his own medicine.

"Mom just fixed some hot cider, Maybelle," June said. "Can you stay a while?"

Maybelle threw off her hat and muff in one motion. "Well, if you really want me to. Just a few minutes, though." She deepened her dimples in Franklin's direction. Franklin backed up against the wall, his beady eyes still hunting for a way to escape. "Oooh, I almost forgot! Silly me!"

She reached into her coat pocket and lifted out a small box wrapped in red foil. A little elf, somewhat flattened, sat on top of the box. June cocked her head to one side. The elf held a little card that read: "To Franklin, Merry Christmas from Merry Maybelle."

To cover her smile, June turned and fastened another gold ball on the tree. Out of the corner of her eye, she watched Maybelle mince across the room to where Franklin was half hidden behind the chair.

"This is for you, Franklin." Maybelle's earrings danced as she shook her head. "I hope you like it."

Franklin held his hands stiffly at his sides. When he opened his mouth to speak, only a croak came out. Recalling his earlier remarks to Whistler, June pushed down the sympathy that automatically rose inside her.

"I guess you're overcome with surprise, huh, Sweetie? Here, I'll open it." Maybelle giggled and winked at June. "I *can* be a little overwhelming—at least, that's what my Henry used to say."

June glanced at Whistler, who grinned back. She could agree with Maybelle about that.

Ripping off the foil, Maybelle produced a bottle of potent after-shave. June could smell it clear across the room. Where on earth did Maybelle get that stuff?

Maybelle held up the bottle, shaped like a barbell. "It's called Muscle Man Cologne. The young salesman assured me that all the men are wearing it."

Whistler rolled his eyes at June and whispered, "I know *one* man who won't be wearing it."

Maybelle removed the cap and waved the open bottle under Franklin's nose, causing him to have an immediate coughing fit. Anne rushed to the kitchen for a glass of water, then helped him to the rocking chair. Maybelle placed the bottle of cologne under the tree—their first present.

When his coughs finally subsided, Franklin sat stiff as a poker and stared at the floor. The odor of Muscle Man Cologne hung heavy in the air. Maybelle leaned against his chair, patting him gently on the back. Franklin looked mad enough to spit.

When Maybelle finally left half an hour later, Franklin glared at June. "You did that on purpose."

"Did what?" June asked innocently.

"Asked her to stay."

June watched Whistler follow her mother into the kitchen, carrying the stacks of dirty cider cups for her. Then she leaned close to Franklin's ear. "Giving a man cologne sounds pretty serious," she whispered. "Maybe I should ask Maybelle about her intentions."

Franklin's head jerked up. "You wouldn't dare."

"You're right. I wouldn't." June paused. "But then," she added softly, "*some* people consider *other* people's feelings."

Just before bedtime, June plodded out in her slippers to get a drink of cold cider. As she drained her glass, voices drifted from the living room. She thought Franklin had gone to bed already. Curious, she slipped into the darkened dining room.

"I can see why Maybelle is a little hard to take," her mom was saying, "but what's wrong with Whistler? He's a nice young man. June seems to have fun with him."

"But not me anymore." Franklin snorted. "I guess playing checkers is too boring for her now."

"That's not true," Anne said soothingly.

"Yes, it is. A young friend is more fun than an old codger." The rocking chair creaked back and forth. "Even a *fat* young friend."

June had felt sorry for Franklin until he said that. Heart fluttering, she entered the living room, stopping directly in front of his rocker. "Whistler isn't fat," she said quietly.

Anne turned a pleading look on Franklin. "I'm sure he didn't mean to insult Whistler. Did you?"

"Yes, I did." Franklin scowled at the floor. "When that fat kid's here, it's too crowded. Can't move in my own house."

"Now, Franklin . . ." Anne began.

"Don't 'now Franklin' me!" he snarled. He flung his skinny arms out, pointing around the room. "Look at all this junk. No place to call my own anymore—oversized tree, and piano books, and boxes of your junk. At least at Reed's I had my own rooms."

June stood there with her mouth open. Franklin wasn't being fair! Why, *he'd* picked out that huge tree himself! It wasn't their fault it took up so much room. And the piano books were inside the bench—they couldn't even be seen! She glanced at her mom and winced. Anne sat like a woman carved from granite; the color had drained from her face.

"Would you like to go back to Reed's? Close up this house again?"

"At least I wasn't useless there!" Eyes flashing, Franklin waved his gnarled hands through the air. "But here I can't cook anything, or clean anything. I can't even water my plants. You beat me to it!" Suddenly exhausted, Franklin fell back against the cushion.

June felt as if her heart had stopped beating. She reached for her mother's hand. It was limp, and cold as ice.

Anne's voice was so soft that June had to lean close

to make out the words. "I just wanted to do a good job. I thought you needed my help. I never meant to get in your way." She sat up straight and, with dignity, announced, "I guess this trial period showed us what we need to know. June and I will pack our things first thing tomorrow."

Leaving Franklin to sit by the flickering lights of the newly decorated Christmas tree, Anne slipped quietly from the room. Feeling as if it were the end of the world, June followed close behind.

June didn't know what was discussed the following day while she was at school, but no more was said about packing and leaving before the trial period was over. The following week the temperature dropped to below zero and stayed there.

However, more than the weather had cooled, June noticed. Ever since the night of the argument, Franklin had been polite to them, but withdrawn. Sometimes he talked with her mom, but with June he was distant. Maybe he was still mad about Maybelle, she thought. He hadn't even asked June to play checkers once all week.

When June awoke on Christmas morning, with carols playing softly over the radio and the aroma of streusel coffee cake warming in the oven, she hoped things would also warm up with Franklin. She'd been surprised, but she missed the quiet talks they had after school, even though there was always more silence than talking. She also missed the endless challenge of trying to beat him at checkers.

When breakfast was over, June quickly passed out the presents from under the tree. In addition to two gifts from her mom and one from Franklin, she had a present from her Aunt Sharon and Uncle Bill. June knew it wasn't nearly as many presents as her friends got, but she knew better than most kids how much they could afford.

"Let's open them one at a time," Anne suggested. "That way it will last a lot longer. June, you start."

June opened the gift from her aunt and uncle first, laughing when she saw a whole box of Hershey bars. She read the note aloud: " 'I know how much you liked these, June. Merry Christmas!' " June glanced up at her mom. "She bought me some candy bars last year at the hospital, remember?"

Next her mom unwrapped two books from her sister, then Franklin opened his gift from Anne—a book on landscaping with hanging plants. June blushed when she opened one gift from her mom, a pink diary, complete with a miniature key. She wondered if her mom could guess what she'd write in it. Next, her mom's gift from Franklin was opened: tiny jars of jellies and jams.

When it was Franklin's turn again, he picked up his package from June. His gnarled fingers worked slowly at the red ribbon tied around it. Finally he lifted the lid and folded back the white tissue paper inside.

For a full thirty seconds, he stared into the box. "What is it?" he finally asked.

June sighed at the suspicious tone of his voice. "A shirt, Franklin."

Anne spoke up quickly. "Hawaiian prints are very fashionable right now."

Franklin reared back as if the colors hurt his eyes. "You expect me to *wear* this?"

"I only wanted to brighten up your black wardrobe." June's voice cracked as she tried to swallow past the lump in her throat.

Franklin held up the flowered shirt with the very ends of his fingertips, as if he couldn't bear to touch a shirt covered with purple and pink hibiscus. "Humph."

June remembered the previous Christmas. "You never wore the scarf I made for you last year either," she mumbled. *And I really slaved over that thing,* she added to herself.

Last year, she'd learned to knit in order to make him a scarf, and it had taken countless hours of her free time—at night, on the playground, in the lunch room, on the school bus. This year, she'd babysat the Jenkins kids four different evenings in order to buy that shirt. After Franklin had looked so out of place at the Father-Daughter Banquet, June had thought he'd appreciate something more fashionable. Evidently not.

"Couldn't you just *pretend* to like it?" June asked, shaking her head. What was the matter with common courtesy, anyway? "You *never* think of my feelings!" Her voice rose shrilly. "It's always the same. You're just old, and . . . and . . . crabby!"

"Oh, June, you don't mean that," her mom whispered anxiously. "Franklin, she doesn't mean that."

Yes, I do, June thought to herself.

Franklin plucked at the sleeve of the flowered shirt and cleared his throat several times. Then, very clumsily, he refolded the shirt and put it back in its box. With a bewildered expression on his face, he looked first at June, then at Anne.

"It's all right," June's mom said, patting his arm and frowning at June.

Suddenly June's anger fizzled as she realized what she'd said. Why had she blurted that out? She'd been hurt, but hurting Franklin back didn't make her feel better. Not one bit.

June stood up abruptly and left the room, still clutching an unopened gift. Softly closing her bedroom door, she sank wearily into her rocking chair near the window.

"What's the matter with me?" she whispered, her breath coming in shallow gasps. "Why did I make such a big deal out of it? It's just a shirt."

Rocking, June let the guilt wash over her in waves. She couldn't forget Franklin's hurt, bewildered expression after her outburst. He didn't understand why she'd exploded. If only he could see that *she* often didn't understand herself these days either! Her mom had promised that mixed-up feelings were normal for a girl her age, but knowing that was no comfort now.

Glancing down, June was surprised to see she still held a tiny wrapped present in her grasp. Turning it over, she saw her name written in a wavering, spidery script. It had to be from Franklin.

Slowly she unwrapped the small velvet-covered, hinged box. When she lifted the lid, June gasped.

There, in a bed of white cotton, lay Ella's rose locket. With trembling fingers, June lifted it from the box and opened it. Two smiling faces looked up at her.

Instead of Franklin and Ella's serious photos, there were now cutouts from snapshots pasted in—one of her mother, and one of her dad. June recalled the day in August when she and her mom had moved in. She'd seen the locket then and wished she could have one like it. Franklin had remembered and granted that wish.

The tears she'd held back now welled up and ran down her cheeks. The smiling faces of her parents blurred.

How could she face Franklin again? She'd accused him of never thinking of her feelings, when all along he'd planned to give her Ella's locket—*his wedding present to her!*

Leaning back in the rocker, June remembered her birthday last year, when Franklin had surprised her with a potted plant—a wild potato. She'd mentioned on a hike once that it was her favorite wildflower, and he'd remembered. It had meant so much to her, a gift given with her especially in mind. The locket she held was the same kind of gift.

Rubbing her forehead, June thought about the hibiscus shirt she'd bought Franklin. Had she really given any thought to what *he* might like for a present? Or had she been more interested in changing his dowdy image? He'd never wanted new, fancier clothes. Biting her lip, June realized he would have probably been happier with a boxful of "organic material" for next year's compost pile.

She wiped the back of her hand across her cheeks and realized she'd been rocking for a long time. The tears had dried. Sighing, she knew what she had to do.

With the locket clutched in her hand, she padded down the hallway, but no sound came from the living room. She peeked around the corner to where Franklin still sat in his chair. Taking a deep breath, she walked over and stood directly in front of him. It took a long time, but she waited until he looked up at her. He stared without a word.

"Um, Franklin, I . . . I . . ." June stopped and cleared her throat, then began again. "I'm sorry about what I said. Really. And I love the locket. It's really special."

Franklin continued to squint at her with black beady eyes, his bushy eyebrows drawn together. As if giving up, he shrugged his bony shoulders and stared back down at his hands. June waited, but he didn't say a word.

She reached out to touch him, hesitated, then pulled her hand back. Turning, June went back to her bedroom. Like two sides of the locket, June's own heart felt nearly split in two.

10

Christmas Dance

❀✿❀

The rest of Christmas passed slowly. Except for Aunt Sharon's call in the morning to wish everyone a Merry Christmas, it was a quiet day. June and Franklin pretended that nothing had happened that morning, but Christmas dinner was strained. By the end of the meal, the conversation was reduced to "Pass the fruit salad" and "Who wants more ham?"

That night June crawled wearily into bed, a feeling of heaviness still weighing her down. Five minutes later, her mom knocked on the door. "Going to sleep already?"

June nodded. "I'm awfully tired. Maybe I'll read for a while first."

Her mom sat on the bed and brushed June's bangs back off her forehead. "I'm sorry about this morning."

"It wasn't your fault. I don't know what got into

me." June slumped back against her pillow. "I wish I could take the words back."

"I know." Anne tucked the quilt up under June's chin. "It's not the end of the world, though. All families rub each other the wrong way sometimes. It'll be fine tomorrow." June's mom kissed her lightly, then patted her shoulder before leaving.

Too tired to read after all, June snapped off her bedside light. Moonlight streamed through the window, softly lighting the room. Padding over to the window, she knelt there and rested her head on her folded arms. Outside, the moon reflected off the powdery snow as if sequins had been sprinkled across the yard. The bare tree branches cast crooked black shadows on the snow drifts.

The scene was so peaceful, so still, that it gradually melted the ache inside her.

Although the backyard was blanketed with snow, June could point to the exact spots where she and Franklin had planted the iris and daffodil bulbs. That fall day had been the first time Whistler had stopped by. June still remembered the shock she'd felt. It was hard to believe that in two days she'd be going to the Christmas dance with him. Even if Whistler wasn't a real boyfriend, his friendship was important to June.

June shifted her weight and tucked her nightgown more tightly around her sore knees. The wood floor was cold, but she hated to go back to bed. She knew she wouldn't sleep for hours yet.

How she wished she'd taken her mom's simple advice from the beginning. If only she'd accepted Franklin exactly the way he was. She could have saved herself a lot of disappointment.

It wasn't as if Franklin had no good points, June reminded herself. She knew he cared about her—he just had funny ways of showing it. Embarrassed as she'd been, June suspected Franklin only questioned Whistler on his "intentions" because he worried about her.

And he *had* surprised her with banquet tickets, June admitted. They'd made an odd-looking couple, but at least he'd brought her favorite dress for her to wear. It wasn't his fault that he'd forgotten to bring the right shoes. Dressing in style had never been Franklin's concern.

And, of course, there was the locket. . . .

Rubbing her cold hands, June decided that Franklin's blunt remarks were the hardest to take. He still embarrassed her when he blurted out exactly what was on his mind. And yet, June knew that some people would call it honesty. Not very *tactful*, maybe, but honest.

Shivering, June finally crawled to her feet. One leg had gone to sleep and felt like a wooden stump. Rubbing the muscles, she padded down to the bathroom for a drink of water. A soft glow from the tree lights filtered down the hall from the living room.

June tiptoed down the hall and peeked around the corner. Franklin sat slumped in his rocker by the piano, head bowed nearly to his chest. June couldn't tell if he was asleep or not.

A floorboard creaked when she shifted, and his head jerked up. "Sorry to scare you," June said, hanging back in the doorway. "Were you asleep?"

Franklin shook his head. "Just thinking."

"What about?" June prompted.

For a full minute Franklin stared at the twinkling tree lights. "You said I'd never change." He kneaded his hands together as if they were numb with cold. His voice was so low June could barely make out the words. "I thought you already liked me. Isn't that why you moved in with me?"

"Oh, Franklin." June went to sit beside him on the floor, tucking his blanket closely around his legs. "Of course it is."

Franklin plucked at the tassels on the blanket. "It's hard to change."

"Don't change," June said firmly. "You have the right to be yourself. It's not my job to make you over."

June thought back to the months of visiting Franklin at the retirement ranch during the foster grandparent program. It had taken the whole school year for him to warm up at all. Even then, he'd still been blunt, but she hadn't minded so much. She'd been happy just to play checkers with him or go on hikes to identify wild-flowers. She had appreciated him just the way he was. Somewhere along the line, she'd lost that.

"Last year it was enough not to be alone all the time. I only wanted your company. Then Mom was sick, and we had to sell the house. I never wanted to move to Cincinnati." June glanced around the cozy room. "I was so excited when you asked us to stay here with you instead."

Franklin spoke slowly, almost as if to himself. "Last year an old woman died in the apartment next to mine.

117

She was all alone. Clara found her in the morning." He shook his head. "No one wants to spend their last hours alone."

"That's why you wanted us to move in with you?"

"Partly. And I liked being with Anne and you. I'd been alone so long."

June remembered the old faded photograph of his wife, Ella. Franklin rarely spoke of her, but she had sounded special.

Franklin stared at the tree lights, as if hypnotized. "When Ella died, I decided it was better to be alone than ever to lose someone again. I didn't want to care about anyone ever again." He paused, his breathing shallow and rapid. "Then you came to visit, and kept coming. You and Anne made me care."

June patted his bony arm, not knowing what to say. Franklin so rarely shared his feelings with her—she hated to break the spell.

He lay his gnarled hand over June's. "I guess I got set in my ways, living all alone. I'm not sure I can change now, even if I try hard."

Shivering, June pulled herself to her feet. "It's getting late. We'd probably better go to bed." She steadied the rocker so he could get up, then unplugged the tree lights. "Don't change, Franklin. That's where I was wrong, and I'm sorry. I *do* like you."

"But?"

"No buts. I like you just the way you are—no strings attached."

The day after Christmas June went shopping with her mom for her first pair of panty hose. June enjoyed wading through the crowds of shoppers, there to snap up after-Christmas specials.

Hunting through a sale bin of packaged hose marked "two for a dollar," June found a pair and grabbed it. "This one's marked Size Small."

"Better look for a 'Petite,' " her mom said, grabbing another pair.

A tiny old lady beside her tried to snatch it out of her hands, but June's mom held tight. Grinning, June followed her mom to the checkout line.

The next afternoon June began to get ready for the dance right after lunch, even though Whistler wasn't to pick her up till seven. Earlier she'd scribbled a long list of things to do: wash hair, paint fingernails, iron dress, polish shoes, take bubble bath, and get dressed. June felt it was crucial that she be ready before Whistler arrived. Although *she* accepted Franklin's right to be himself, she wasn't sure she could expect her friends to feel the same way.

By six o'clock June's hair was curled, and her red fingernails matched the trim on her freshly ironed dress. After soaking in the tub, her wrinkled toes looked like pink raisins. With one eye on the clock, she grabbed a clean gym sock and vigorously polished her patent leather shoes with the one-inch heels.

"June, come eat a bite!" her mom called. "You don't want to faint at the dance."

In the kitchen, wrapped in a terry bathrobe, June

tried to force down her sandwich. The tuna lodged in her throat, and her stomach seemed to jump from side to side, as if it couldn't make up its mind where to settle.

"When's your young man coming?" Franklin asked.

June glanced over her shoulder at the clock. "He'll be here in half an hour!" Eyes wide in alarm, she held up her half-eaten sandwich.

"Don't worry. There's plenty of time to get ready. You don't have to finish your sandwich if you don't want it."

"Thanks." Pushing back her chair, June raced to the bathroom and grabbed her toothbrush. The last thing she needed tonight was tuna stuck in her teeth.

Back in her bedroom, she carefully pulled the new panty hose from the package. Dismayed, she held them up. "Mom! Oh, Mom!"

"What is it? What's wrong?" her mom asked, hurrying into the room.

"Look!" She held up the crushed, wrinkled hose by the waistband. From top to bottom, they only measured about twelve inches. "A midget couldn't squeeze into these. I guess we should have bought the small size, not the petite."

"Put them on. They'll fit." At June's skeptical frown, her mom smiled. "Trust me."

Perched on the end of the bed, June carefully pushed her legs into the hose. She was relieved to see they really stretched. With a little wiggling, they soon reached all the way to her waist. "I guess you were right," she said sheepishly.

"Here. Let me help you with your dress." Anne slipped the crisp material over June's head, careful not to muss her sprayed curls held back by a lacy red bow. "Hold still now. Let me zip you."

June craned her neck to see her bedside clock. "*Hurry*, Mom. It's ten till seven. He'll be here any minute. I've *got* to beat Franklin to the door when Whistler gets here."

"There, that's it." Anne Finch finished the last button on June's cuffs, then fastened the locket at her neck. "Turn around now, and let me see you."

Suddenly shy and self-conscious, June pivoted slowly on her heel.

"Oh, honey, your dad would have been so proud." Her mom smiled brightly, but June saw the tears brimming in her eyes.

"Well, I'd better get out to the living room," June said. "I don't want . . ." The chiming of the doorbell interrupted her. "Oh, no, he's here!" June yelled to the kitchen where Franklin was washing up the supper dishes. "It's okay, Franklin, I'll get it."

With a last look in the mirror, she scooted down the hall. Unfortunately, she hadn't reckoned with her patent leather shoes. Still slick on the bottom, they sent her skidding as she rounded the corner. Thrown off balance, June grabbed the antique wooden trunk that had been made into a table. As she caught herself, her leg brushed against a splinter on the trunk. A horrid tingling sensation ran from her calf right up to her waist.

"Oh, no." Groaning, June stared at the long run that had made a stripe up the side of her leg. "Oh, *no*."

The doorbell rang again, but she spun on her heel and raced back down the hall. "Mom!"

"What happened?"

"Look!" June pulled up her skirt and stuck out her leg.

The doorbell rang a third time, and June heard Franklin stomp into the living room. The front door opened and closed, but their voices were too faint to hear at the back of the house.

It was exactly what June had been afraid of. "Mom, please go talk to Whistler until I get out there. Don't let Franklin say anything awful to him."

"But what about your run? Don't you need my help?"

Close to tears, June collapsed on the bed and kicked off her shoes. "Do you have some hose I could borrow?"

"Of course, but they may not fit you very well." She hurried across the hall to her own room. Thirty seconds later she was back. "How about these? They're a bit baggy, but I think they'll do."

June stripped off her ruined hose, then jammed her feet into her mom's pair and quickly pulled them up. They lay in wrinkled brown folds around her thin ankles.

"Try stretching them further."

"Okay." After yanking on the elastic top, the panty hose reached nearly to her armpits. June looked at her mom in despair.

"They'll work fine, honey. No one will know." Anne Finch gently placed her cool hands on the sides of June's face. "Are you ready to go now?" she asked.

June nodded, then slipped on her shiny shoes again. Wishing she could crawl under her quilt and stay there forever, June instead forced herself to leave the bedroom. Her slow, careful steps barely made a sound in the hall. At the living-room doorway, the conversation she overheard made her catch her breath.

"How was your Christmas?" Franklin was asking. "Lots of good food?"

"Yup! That's my favorite part. The holidays are no time to diet though!" Whistler smacked his lips. "Ham, turkey, and mincemeat pies!"

June closed her eyes, praying desperately that Franklin wouldn't tell Whistler he resembled a stuffed turkey himself. She glided into the living room before Franklin could answer.

Whistler jumped to his feet. In his tan slacks and dark brown sweater and tie, June thought he looked like a giant teddy bear. "Hi, Whistler," she murmured, suddenly shy.

"Hi. You look real nice, June."

"Thanks." June turned to get her coat, but stopped in amazement.

"You do look nice," Franklin agreed.

June stared openmouthed. Her reply stuck in her throat. She couldn't take her eyes off Franklin as he shuffled toward her. He wore black shoes, black pants, and the pink and purple flowered shirt that June had given him for Christmas. Still wrinkled and creased from the package, it hung loosely on his thin frame.

June reached up to kiss his withered cheek. "You look dashing too," she whispered. "Want to take me to the dance instead?"

Blushing, Franklin's face soon matched the pink hibiscus. "Harrumph." Reaching deep into his baggy trouser pocket, he fished around for two quarters and handed them to Whistler. "You and June go out for ice cream on the way home. My treat."

June winked at her mom while she slipped on her coat. Franklin didn't go out much. He didn't know fifty cents wouldn't even buy one cone at the Ice Kream Korner.

"Thank you, Sir." Whistler shook his hand. "Well, Dad's waiting outside to drive us. We should go."

June zipped her parka self-consciously. "Well, bye, Mom. Bye, Franklin."

"Bye, honey. Have a good time."

Whistler held the door for June, then followed her outside and helped her down the slippery porch steps. "You know," he said, "Franklin's not a bad old guy."

June stopped at the sidewalk and looked back. With the curtains pulled aside, Franklin and her mom watched from the front window. Her mom waved, but Franklin stood stiffly dignified in his hibiscus shirt.

"You're right," June agreed. "Franklin *is* a neat guy, but he's more than that. He's family." With a wave, she turned toward the car parked at the curb.